"We Look Rather Well Together. . . .

Yes, her fairness and his dark suntanned looks perfectly complemented each other. In the mirror they had looked like young lovers on the very brink of fulfillment. . . .

What would it feel like to be in his arms, close as close could be to this man with the mocking, heart-stopping smile?

Angry at him and at her own too vivid thoughts, Penny pushed herself up from the bed.

"Is *this* why you hire girls to travel with you?" she rasped. "Is this the real reason you gave me a job? My pay is Vienna . . . and *you?*"

JULIET ASHBY
lives in Philadelphia, but loves to travel and especially adores Paris. After working as a newspaper reporter—like her father, grandfather and husband—she is now a novelist. She confesses to a weakness for pastels, old French furniture and Renoir paintings; and has two sons, one of whom is a classical violinist.

Dear Reader:

I'd like to take this opportunity to thank you for all your support and encouragement of Silhouette Romances.

Many of you write in regularly, telling us what you like best about Silhouette, which authors are your favorites. This is a tremendous help to us as we strive to publish the best contemporary romances possible.

All the romances from Silhouette Books are for you, so enjoy this book and the many stories to come. I hope you'll continue to share your thoughts with us, and invite you to write to us at the address below:

Karen Solem
Editor-in-Chief
Silhouette Books
P.O. Box 769
New York, N.Y. 10019

JULIET ASHBY
One Man Forever

Silhouette *Romance*
Published by Silhouette Books New York
America's Publisher of Contemporary Romance

To Jonathan

SILHOUETTE BOOKS, a Simon & Schuster Division of
GULF & WESTERN CORPORATION
1230 Avenue of the Americas, New York, N.Y. 10020

Distributed by Pocket Books

ISBN: 0-671-57162-1

First Silhouette Books printing July, 1982

10 9 8 7 6 5 4 3 2 1

Map by Tony Ferrara

America's Publisher of Contemporary Romance

Printed in the U.S.A.

One Man Forever

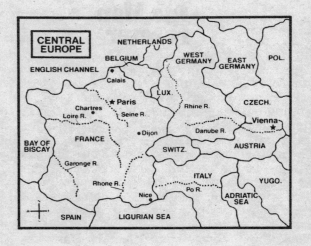

Chapter One

"I'm sorry, Mr. Bannister, I can *barely* hear you!" Penny Marsh cried into the telephone. Cupping one hand over her ear, she strained to catch the voice traveling the transatlantic cables from London. There were two reasons she was having trouble: one was the lively action going on in the auction room just off the corridor, and the other was the action going on 3000 miles away—she thought she could distinctly hear Big Ben tolling the hour in Westminster Tower.

"Could you please speak up, Mr. Bannister?" she cried again, her pale, heart-shaped face twisted in anxiety.

"I *said*," the cultured British voice suddenly shed its grace and turned gravelly, "I said you're dismissed! You're sacked! You've made me lose the one thing I was determined to acquire—that Amati! I *told* you I had to have it! I *told* you to query me if you ran into any problem!"

"I tried! I couldn't get through. We lost the connection!" Penny struggled to hold back the

7

hot tears. "Besides, the man who got it went five thousand over your figure! I've got your letter right here. I stuck to your high bid!"

"I never meant that to be an absolute, just a guideline. I tell you, young lady, it's a good thing you're across the ocean or I'd . . . I'd take you to the Tower and watch your head roll!"

Trembling, Penny stared at the telephone. Although small and delicately put together, she had a very firm spine, and now she drew herself up to her full height of five feet three inches. "Mr. Bannister, I'm *glad* you didn't get that violin! I'd rather see it in the hands of . . . of . . . an *orangutan!*"

She slammed the phone down, ablaze with anger—but not just for the employer she had never seen; she was every bit as angry at Penny Marsh. Penny Marsh, who needed a job and had muffed her first assignment. Why hadn't she made absolutely certain in advance how high the man had been willing to bid?

"Your literary allusions are a little mixed up, aren't they?"

She turned, startled by a deep voice. Then she stiffened, her turquoise eyes turning cold as a winter lake.

He was leaning against a shelf of tattered phone books, smiling—no, smirking. "I believe the reference goes something like this: 'a man making love to a woman is like an orangutan playing the violin.' But no matter, I'm sure the party at the other end of the phone got your general unflattering gist."

"Do you eavesdrop on other people's phone conversations often?" Penny groped around the darkened booth for her purse. "I don't know how you even have the nerve to *talk* to me! *You're* the reason I lost my job! I practically had that violin wrapped and ready to go. You stole in with your bid at the very last second! It was just so . . . so darned unfair!"

"Really?" The condescending smile on his full lips broadened. "Since when is it the custom to broadcast when one intends to bid?" His eyes traveled over her almost as if *she* were up for auction. "Who's your principal by the way? Did I hear you say Bannister? You represent old Edward T.?"

"*Used* to represent! But I can't imagine why you think I want to discuss this with *you!*" Darting out of the booth, she deftly circled him, her blue and plum pleated skirt awhirl. Abruptly she was conscious of the man's disturbing quality, the lustrous dark eyes that would not be intimidated, but followed her with a kind of mocking awareness of her femininity. One thing Penny had learned in her admittedly sheltered twenty-one years was that there were two kinds of men walking around the globe: the boy-next-door type, who treated girls as if they really were sugar and spice and everything nice, and the other kind, the ones who looked on every female as a personal challenge, a mystery to be solved, a mountain peak that had to be scaled—because it was there. There was something about the eyes of the latter type, eyes that probed deep into

9

the heart of a girl's womanliness . . . dangerous eyes, the eyes of a sheik in a romantic movie.

"I find it rather surprising that old E.T. would leave the purchase of something as valuable as an Amati to the judgment of an inexperienced school girl, someone so obviously unused to auctions." His voice was aimed at her back.

Penny spun around, the brief flash of her anger whipping into a hurricane. It was too much, being made to feel a fool twice in one morning! "Listen, you got what you wanted, didn't you? You own the violin. So now go lock it up in your vault! That's what you slick investors do with fine instruments, isn't it? A violin's just so many dollar bills to you people!"

Did she imagine she'd punctured his suavity? Did the intense sheik's eyes widen, alter in some way? But then she saw the sardonic twist of his lips. "Ah, a romantic! Not a helpful characteristic if you intend to make auctions your line, my dear. Buying at auctions is not an endeavor for the sensitive."

"I fully believe *that!*" she said scornfully and swept down the dusty corridor and around the corner, into Passman's buzzing auction room.

"Now Number 124," the auctioneer was saying hoarsely from his lectern. "Painted tinware: this rare, lace-edged tray, earliest made in America, right after the Revolution. Multiflowered, excellent condition. I'm starting at five thousand. Do I hear a bid?"

Penny edged around the eager crowd of women collectors who had been waiting all morning for this moment. They stretched their necks to stare avidly at the tray, chirping like birds at a picnic. She found one of the few empty chairs and sank into it, only half listening to the auctioneer's chant. "I see five-six . . . I see five-seven . . ."

She didn't know why she was lingering. There was no point now. Except that in a few minutes they'd be auctioning a very fine violin bow and she was curious to see how much it would draw. She would have loved to make a bid herself, but, of course, that was laughable. She had barely enough money to cover her living expenses for the rest of the month.

And after that, what?

Fighting the rush of panic, she told herself, the thing to do is go home, eat lunch, calm down and then do some stern cold thinking, set yourself a course of action.

You definitely will *not* mope!

Yet she couldn't seem to stir. The truth was, she hated the thought of returning to the skimpily furnished bedroom-kitchenette that had been her home for the past two months. Everytime she unlocked the door she remembered that other apartment—the charming, bay-windowed place near the historic district of Philadelphia that she and Linda had planned on sharing. It had been on the second floor of the building they had rented to house their little business, Penlin's Antic Antiques . . . the business that had never opened its doors.

Her lips quivered as she recalled the day an

artist friend had created the sign for them, executed in old English lettering. "See? It's Penny and Linda combined, Penlin's. Isn't that cute, don't you just *love* it?" Linda's pretty face had been alive with enthusiasm.

The two girls had dreamed about opening the shop all through their senior year at college. They'd spent all their combined resources to pay three months' advance rent, and all their energies cleaning, painting and papering. Their stock had consisted of an ancient rocking chair donated by Linda's grandmother, and some worn silver pieces from Penny's family. "This will be an antique shop with a personality!" Linda had declared. "An antique shop known for its *antics!* We'll give high teas, read poetry, dress up in Revolutionary costumes—maybe they'll feature us on TV! Oh, Penny, it's going to be such *fun!*"

Fun. Had all the fun in the world died with Linda? Penny thought now with a shudder. Suddenly she felt unbearably alone—an odd feeling to be having, sitting in this crowded auction house with all the excited yelps and squeals and whispers going on around her.

She had begun the day with such hope. The chance to work for E.T. Bannister of London had seemed the ideal job for her. But she had muffed things on the first assignment. And how many jobs of that nature—bidding on musical instruments—existed in the world? She'd gotten the connection only because an old friend of her father's had glowingly recommended her. "I told

Bannister you were the perfect U.S. contact," her father's friend had written. "As the daughter of David Ernst Marsh you were trained from an early age to know fine instruments."

But what good was training that had no market? And how many Mr. Bannisters were there, men who could afford to pay someone to buy fine things for them?

"I see the Tourte bow's next on the agenda."

Penny stiffened. She didn't even have to look, she knew that voice. Lips tightening, she raised herself up out of her chair. Pointedly she scanned the room for a vacant seat.

"Miss, sit down! I can't *see!*" an indignant white-haired lady hissed from behind.

"Full house today," murmured Penny's bedeviler, heavy eyebrows peaked amusedly. "Looks as if you'll just have to stay where you are and suffer."

"Suffer is an absolutely *perfect* word!" Flushed and frustrated, Penny sank back in her chair, locked in by his long legs on one side and a bulky lady in a bulkier Persian lamb coat on the other.

"All right, ladies and gentlemen, we come to Number 125." The auctioneer's broad smile seemed incongruous over his funereal black suit. "A Xavier Tourte bow, period 1770–1786, authenticating papers from Hill, London. I'm starting with twenty-five thousand—"

"Unbelievable—that price's shot up like a missile," said the man whose shoulder nudged Penny's, intentionally, she was sure.

13

"Well, it *is* a Tourte," she said coldly. "You couldn't find a more marvelous bow." With an elaborate shudder, she moved her shoulder from his.

The mocking eyes surveyed her. They were set in lashes so thick they tangled. Men with long lashes, Penny thought, could never be trusted. "Is that an expert opinion?" he asked.

"It's not an opinion, it's a statement of fact."

"And what precisely distinguishes this bow? I mean, seeing that you're so knowledgeable."

"Well, from a physical standpoint, there's the fleur-de-lis on each side of the frog and—"

"I should think the first thing you would mention would be that it was once in the Paris collection of Georges Hembert."

"Wrong!" Penny shot the word at him with a spurt of delight. "You're talking about the *François* Tourte bow. This is *Xavier* Tourte!"

"You're sure about that?" Frowning, he bent over the catalogue in his lap. "Suppose we check and see what the real experts say."

There was a long moment of silence.

"Well?" Penny stabbed.

"Er . . . you have apparently checked your catalogue more precisely than I." His voice was gruff.

"I didn't have to check anything so elementary! I just happen to know about violins—*care* about them. I'm sure you find that difficult to understand!" She jumped up, relishing his flushed face. "Now, if you'll just let me through—"

He moved his long legs aside, and Penny squeezed past, pushing into the aisle. Passman's was having a record day; it took almost ten minutes to work her way to the back exit, and by that time the bidding on the bow was well under way. It was going to be a quick sale, she could tell from the bidding. She glanced at the lectern. "Twenty-five—twenty-five—twenty-five," the auctioneer was saying. "Over there, twenty-six. This is your last chance. Anyone?" The hammer struck. "Sold to the gentleman in the handsome tweeds, one of our favorite customers, Mr.—"

A burst of noise obliterated the rest of it, but Penny saw the gentleman—*gentleman?*—in the handsome tweeds making his way to the desk to claim his prize.

Buying an Amati violin and a Tourte bow in one morning! He must have struck oil under his front porch! she thought sourly. *One of those characters who puts himself to sleep counting the banks in which he has deposits! He buys up violins for their dollar value—play a Strad and he won't hear a note, but rustle a hundred-dollar bill and he'll think it's the heavenly choir!*

Wasn't it strange that men like that, men who were arrogant and drivingly ambitious, were so often blessed by the gods with such vibrant male beauty? Now that she was away from him, she realized with surprise that her bidding competitor was what the girls at college had called a "Wow Specimen." Thick straight hair, mahogany brown shot with sparks of gold, a clean, knife-edged profile, plunging perceptive eyes, a mouth . . . *sumptuous* was the word that came to mind when she thought of that long, full mouth.

She stamped out to Passman's cluttered foyer, not letting herself stop to examine the marvelous gold Queen Anne chair an employee was ticketing. Queen Anne chairs had been a favorite of Linda's, and Penny didn't want to think about her old friend and the heartless man who had caused her death.

But suddenly she realized that Linda's man and the arrogant man she had just encountered were of the same breed, brothers under the skin! "Never fall in love with a man who's power mad," Linda had said once, "he'll drive *you* mad." Linda had laughed to lighten the dramatic prophecy, but she had been right, horribly right. One night, distraught after an argument with her power mad lover—who apparently had a girl for every day in the week—Linda had turned to avoid an oncoming car that swerved into her lane and had crashed through the bridge railing and fallen into the relentless, eternal embrace of death.

Yes, Linda's lover and the man in the handsome tweeds were two of a kind, with the same penetrating eyes, the same aura of danger.

Outside on Chestnut Street Penny quickened her steps, while her thoughts scurried and tumbled and darted, whipped by myriad, very real anxieties.

Then all at once she realized the sun had come out and that it had a different feel to it. In a shop window she saw it had presented her with a shimmering halo, left her white-gold hair bright as a crown. Spring . . . at last! Spring meant hope, fresh beginnings, a time to put away drab winter clothes, not to mention winter's gloom and grief.

Darting around the corner, she gave her customary respectful salute to Independence Hall, stately and somehow moving in its red brick square. By the time she reached her apartment, she was humming a vague but cheery tune.

A yellow notice was stuck in her door. It didn't surprise her, she had been told that the landlady frequently presented some kind of demand to complicate life and slenderize the tenants' purses. "As of April 1, the management is requesting a ten percent increase, due to a raise in electric rates."

"Better get stirring, girl," Penny told her image in the hall mirror. For a moment she studied her wind-tossed hair, the large turquoise eyes that had recently acquired a faintly lost look, the pale skin that hinted at sleepless hours.

One reliable pepper upper was a cup of tea, she told herself as she put water on to boil. Another was a session with the paint pots. She turned to the mirror . . . a dab of apricot "instant health" on the cheeks, soft blue eyeshadow, a little pink gloss on the lips . . .

There. Now maybe she looked like someone,

17

somebody, somewhere would hire—for something. The thing was to find the something.

Tackling yesterday's leftover ham sandwich, she scientifically reviewed her vital statistics.

Penny Jeanne Marsh, just turned twenty-one.

Emotional Support Systems: None. Both parents killed in an airplane crash a year before graduation. Three months after graduation, best friend drowned.

Health: Still shaky from the above emotional triple-whammy.

Training: Liberal arts education, a knowledge of musical instruments and antique furniture.

Finances: Close to zero.

Prospects: Even closer.

Summarized, it all looked pretty hopeless, Penny told herself. And it was the absence of just one understanding person that made the difference. Even after her parents' deaths, she had had Linda, her close friend since grade school. Having Linda had made it possible to steer through even the choppiest waters.

How she hated him, the man who had swept Linda to her doom! She could still see him, pulling up to the dorm in his Mercedes. So much older and more sophisticated than Linda. A man who owned his own Cessna and a yacht and a harem of women. . . .

"I just adore him!" Linda had cried, her eyes alive with a frightening, yet somehow thrilling, light.

It must be thrilling to find your man, Penny thought wistfully, to know he would belong only

18

to you, forever—something poor Linda had never felt.

Better to go unloved, Penny thought, than to be involved with that kind of man, a man to whom you'd be just one more territory to conquer! And yet, wasn't it natural to admire a man strong enough to make his mark on the world? Could there be a man somewhere who combined masculine drive and power with endearing sweetness and sensitivity?

Believe that, Penny told herself, *and soon you'll be writing letters to the Easter Bunny!*

She hurried her dishes to the sink, snatched up her coat again. There was a whole world out there that needed millions of simple tasks performed. She could wait tables, sell dresses, demonstrate merchandise at the supermarket!

And, come to think of it, this morning there had been a sign in the little red-and-white candy shop on Spruce Street: SALESGIRL WANTED, APPLY WITHIN.

Who knows? Maybe I have a very special talent for wrapping up a pound of fudge!

She giggled and instantly felt better. She was halfway to the door when the telephone shrilled.

It actually frightened her—no one had phoned in the longest time, because there wasn't anyone *to* phone. She'd been away at college for four years and her precollege friends had scattered to marriage or other cities, or had jobs that took all their time. In fact, her last phone call had been two weeks ago.

No, I don't care to subscribe to the Needle-

work Guide for Nervous Nonentities . . . Sorry, I have no need for a combination potato peeler—nutcracker—can opener—back scratcher . . . And I don't want to buy a ski slope in the Everglades . . .

But the voice on the phone didn't belong to a man who sold things.

It belonged to a man who *bought* things, magnificent things.

A man with a sheik's insolent eyes.

"Miss Marsh, I'm right across the street—I think the place is called the Liberty Bell Sandwich Shop. Not exactly an inspiring atmosphere. Would you consider rescuing me from it?"

Chapter Two

"Sorry about the lack of ambience." He waved a hand at the sandwich shop's smudged plastic tabletops and napkin-strewn floor. "Apparently this is the only place around with a telephone. I didn't want to risk terrifying you by suddenly looming up outside your door." His lips curved in the maddeningly superior way that was beginning to look all too familiar. "Knowing what a sensitive creature you are."

Penny looked narrowly at him. "Would you mind telling me what this is about? How did you get my phone number?"

He reached in the pocket of his tweed coat. Against the background of the Liberty Bell Sandwich Shop Penny thought he looked like a diamond on a five-and-dime counter. And then she saw what he was holding out to her.

"My notebook!" She grabbed it. "How did you get that?"

"You left it in Passman's phone booth. Which is how I came to know your name and address.

Which, via the directory, led quite naturally to your phone number. Satisfactory explanation?"

"Oh. *Oh*. Well . . . thank you! I appreciate . . ." Looking down she saw Mr. Bannister's letter sliding out of the notebook's pages. Had he read it? If so, he knew quite a lot about her personal business. "I suppose you . . ."

"Read Bannister's note?" The knowing smile again. "Frankly—yes."

"But you had no *right* . . ."

"Perhaps not. Except that there was no envelope with the letter, so in order to find out your name and address I had to look at the upper left-hand corner of the letter. And after *that*, I looked up your phone number. And after *that*, I had to walk ten blocks out of my way, *then* wait ten minutes, ten minutes of my work day, for you to get here. So on the basis of my average hourly earning power, you owe me—let's see . . ."

"*I* owe *you!*" she cried, and then, realizing his eyes were laughing at her, she simmered down a little. "Well, look, if you can find me a job, maybe I'll be able to repay you for all your trouble! Although actually I'd say *you* owe *me*. You've lost me one job and if I don't move fast, I'll lose a chance at another."

His smile faded. Darting her a quick, tight look, he picked up his coat. "What I should have done was simply chuck that notebook in the nearest trash bin."

"Oh—oh, I'm *sorry!* I really shouldn't have . . ." All at once she felt whirled about, flooded with embarrassment. He *had* done her a favor. She wouldn't have wanted her notebook found by just anyone. But she wished it hadn't been him. Mr. Bannister's letter—so personal— commenting on her father's career and subsequent illness, making references to her own background . . . And now she remembered she'd been trying to draw up a budget—the notebook listed her financial assets and liabilities. All in all, a telling, humiliating find.

Carefully she tucked the notebook in her purse. "It was thoughtful of you to bring this. Thank you."

"Ah, that's an improvement. Yes, much more acceptable." His manner was annoyingly lordly.

"What do you mean by that?"

"Strictly complimentary, I assure you. I was enjoying the glimpse of your gentler nature. Like the sky after a chilling rainstorm, it surprises and relieves."

Her lips tightened. Obviously he was mocking her, but it couldn't possibly matter, since *he* didn't matter. "Well, thank you again, Mr.—"

He rose. "I'm Pierce Reynolds."

Instantly a tall white tower rose in Penny's mind, the Reynolds Building, where stocks and bonds exchanged hands and international trade flourished, and Pierce Reynolds daily added to his success as an investor. PIERCE REYNOLDS, A NEW BREED, THE UNDER-40 SUPER ACHIEVER, a newsmagazine had proclaimed on its scarlet cover just a few weeks ago.

"How do you do?" She spoke coolly, determined not to show she was in any way impressed. "And now I simply must run!"

Which she did. She was across the luncheonette's grimy tiles and yanking at the door when a tanned hand stretched around her and held it for her. "You know," he said, "you've just given me a rather intriguing idea."

His face was only inches from her own. It was annoying, the way that flustered her. It was the mouth . . . so full and sensuous, and yet with such sharply indented edges. A mouth that could bark commands—and be cruel and possessive with a woman.

The thought, stealing from nowhere, angered her. "Mr. Reynolds, I don't want to be rude, but I *am* on my way to see about a job."

"Oh? Doing what?"

Had the man no sense that he was intruding? She let out an impatient sigh. "Oh, nothing, selling fudge!" She moved around the door.

"Fudge?" He followed, planting himself in front of her.

"I'm sure you've heard of it—the fattening chocolate stuff men gobble and girls only dream about!" She laughed nervously. "Now, please, if you'll just let me by . . ." She made a placating smile.

"First I'd like to talk to you a minute."

She pretended not to hear. She strode past him, went a few paces, then broke into an impulsive run. She tore across the street just as the light changed, almost colliding with a half-

block-long truck with WILSON—PIANO MOVERS
on its heavy flank. Panting, she zigzagged,
ducked into an alley, skittered across Locust
Street to Spruce.

All the while conscious of a small, satisfied
smile on her lips.

She could still see the startled lift of his eyebrows. A girl running away from him! It must
have been a surprising new experience!

I'm Pierce Reynolds. He'd said it as if he
expected trumpets to sound, expected her to
stand and gape. Self-absorbed, just like Linda's
man. Linda's man, who had kept poor Linda
nervously waiting on every date.

Ah, there it was, Candyland's red-and-white-
striped awning. And the SALESGIRL WANTED
sign still on the door! Such a pretty little shop to
start your career in fudge—was this why she'd
worked so hard to get summa cum laude on her
diploma?

And then the practical side of her nature
asserted itself. It *would* be nice to have a salary
and a packed grocery shelf, maybe even a new
blouse. Her college wardrobe was wearing very
thin, she hadn't bought anything since her parents' deaths.

No, don't think about that, she told herself.
*You're going into that shop looking like the
blue bird of happiness. They don't want sour-
faced people selling their fudge.*

Sleighbells tinkled over her head, the rich
scrumptious aroma of chocolate filled her nos-

trils, and she thought, *it's going to be my lucky day, I know it!*

There was only one customer, a lady in a feathered hat who seemed to be browsing among the chocolate-covered nuts.

"I came about the job!" Penny blurted eagerly at the proprietor, a pleasant-faced elderly man in a bow tie.

"Didn't I take down that sign?" The man shook his head regretfully. "I'm sorry, Miss, just hired a young lady."

At that moment the young lady, a thin redhead, emerged from the back of the shop bearing a rather awkwardly wrapped package.

The proprietor, tsk-tsking, moved to the door to take down the SALESGIRL WANTED sign. As Penny trudged out again, he called, "Sorry."

"Me too," she said wanly. *So I'll never be another Fannie Farmer,* she thought. But it was hard to be really jaunty, not only because she had lost out, but because the delicious aroma of fudge was stirring a million longing juices in her digestive system. Her tiny lunch seemed light years ago.

If a whiff of chocolate does this to you, it's a good thing the job was taken, she thought, *in a year you'd be a perfect blimp.*

"Actually, that wasn't your kind of atmosphere, those red and white stripes just weren't you."

From somewhere he swung alongside her, shortening his steps to match hers. Penny gave him a quick, indignant look and then realized he wasn't making fun of her, his expression was sympathetic, as if he were trying to soften the edges of her frustration.

"The whole situation wouldn't sit right, anyway," he said, "David Ernst Marsh's daughter dispensing fudge."

"How do you know . . . ? Oh . . . oh, the letter."

"Plus the resemblance. I saw your father once, a long time ago; he was playing with the Philadelphia Orchestra. Stately looking man, a marvelous musician. How come he retired so young?"

Penny bit her lip. "He wasn't actually young, just looked it. He married very late, too."

"Well, I guess to you the whole world must seem old, present company included. What are you, nineteen? Oh, no, you're a college grad. Twenty-two. And pristine as springtime."

"Twenty-*one*. And at the moment I feel much more like winter—a bleak, cold, horrible one with a leak in the roof!" She dug her hands in her pockets. "And Dad retired because he developed arthritis, the worst thing that could happen to a violinist."

"I should imagine it would be devastating."

"Yes, financially, too. They never told me how rough things got for them. I never knew they were selling things. They even mortgaged the house—just for me, just to keep me in college and . . . and fashionably dressed . . . and . . . and . . . *blind!*" Tears abruptly burned her

27

eyes. "I don't understand why they didn't tell me. Why didn't they realize I'd rather have *them* any day?"

"I imagine they wanted you to have the chance to develop your potential, the intelligence that's so obviously in you."

Surprised, she glanced at him and then she was suffused with embarrassment. He was being outwardly polite, but covering up what he had to be thinking—that she was a babbling idiot, spilling out such intimate feelings to a total stranger!

"Hi, Pierce darling!"

The voice floated in the air, light as a balloon. A tall fashionable girl who looked like a model was passing in the opposite direction—a gorgeous, long-limbed brunette in a Norwegian blue-fox jacket. Her dark eyes laughed in Pierce Reynolds' direction, as if reliving happy memories.

Over the heads of the shoppers he called, "Oh, hello there, Barb," and smiled briefly.

Something about the casual response infuriated Penny—the king bestowing recognition on a lowly subject. Was the girl an ex-love he'd tired of? How she hated ladies' men!

She stopped abruptly, nodding toward the opposite corner. "Here's where I take off."

He caught her arm. "Not this time."

Suddenly she was smelling a fragrance, a whiff of something spicy, captivating, some designer's very masculine, very expensive cologne for men.

And in her mind's eye she saw the fluted bottle of *Adored* sitting on her dresser. A boy at college had given it to her for Christmas, and she'd never even opened it.

I ought to use perfume more often. I really ought to make it part of my daily grooming.

The thought left her furious with herself. Perfume—why on earth was she thinking about something as trivial as perfume?

And why, in her troubled circumstances, was she strolling along Locust Street as if she had all the time in the world . . . strolling with this stranger?

Hurriedly she disentangled her arm from her escort's, at the same time sharply aware of the commanding quality of his profile, the broad rugged solidity of his shoulders. The magazine article had hinted that his women dotted the globe like so many pushpins in a map—and who wanted to be a pushpin?

"Let's begin some serious talk now," Pierce Reynolds was saying. "You're in need of a job, right?"

"Only the way I need oxygen! So if you'll excuse me . . ."

"Now, listen—since I contributed to putting you among the unemployed . . ."

"Oh, that's done now. I wasn't really on the beam, anyway."

"Agreed. But I'm sure you can learn. In fact, I have an intuitive feeling about you, and I never argue with my intuition."

She felt his gaze wandering over her, apprais-

29

ing, assessing . . . and once again she felt a tremulous, puzzling self-consciousness. He was so different from most men—complex, secretive. . . .

"Look," he said, "you play the violin, I presume?"

"Yes, but not in any way that would interest Carnegie Hall! It's just a hobby."

"Yes, I find it easy to picture you with a violin." He looked thoughtful for a moment. "Yes . . . yes, the more I think of it . . . Look, let's you and I find a quiet table at The Fernery while I talk you into flying to Vienna with me."

Penny felt her mouth fall open. Had she heard what she knew she'd heard? Indignation rose in her like fumes in a volcano and at the same time she was feeling the most inexplicable impulse. . . .

She wanted to straighten his tie.

Such a senseless thing, how that slightly off-center tie bothered her! Why should it matter?

"I hope you like Rob Roys," he was saying. "The Fernery turns out the best Rob Roy on the Eastern Seaboard." He stated it as if it were an unalterable fact instead of simply his opinion.

"Mr. Reynolds," she backed away from him, her eyes as frosty as she could make them, "I'm getting a very funny feeling here. As if somebody's trying to . . . would the word be *seduce*? —somebody."

Mocking laughter showed in his eyes, and as his gaze roved over her she felt her throat tighten—was it apprehension, excitement? "I can see," he murmured, "that somebody might be tempted to embark on such an endeavor with somebody."

"Well, sorry to disappoint you, and this may sound really old-fashioned, but I'm *not* that kind of girl!"

He laughed. "I suspected that. But frankly, why do you assume so much? You're putting things on a rather personal level."

"A personal level! What could be more personal than asking a girl to fly to Vienna with you?"

"Hmm . . ." his eyes were maddening, teasing, "yes, I guess that *could* sound somewhat personal—if your thoughts move in that direction."

"Look, I suppose you think because you're Pierce Reynolds I should be bowing down to you or . . . or fainting with gratitude! Well, I have news for you, if this is your way of amusing yourself—to me your type is a pure, absolute turnoff!"

"What brings all this about?" He stood silently looking at her defiant expression for a long moment, and then gave a kind of weary sigh and looked away, his mouth tightening, his eyes turning remote. "All right, Miss Marsh, let's go back to square one. I'm talking about a job for you. I'm certainly not expecting you to bow down, and I never seduce infants. When I ask you to go to Vienna with me, there is nothing in the least personal about it. I need a job done, and I have the feeling you are the person to handle it."

"You're talking about work? Pure nine-to-five, sweat-of-the-brow labor?"

"I certainly have no reason to talk to you about anything else." His voice was cold, his eyes flat. Oddly bothered, Penny stared at the pavement. *No reason to talk to you about anything else.* Well, of course, how ridiculous she must have sounded . . . a man who had girls like the long-legged brunette in the Norwegian fox. Why would he have designs on an ordinary Penny Marsh type?

The only role he sees you in is that of a slave, she told herself, *one of his many time-clock punchers.*

But then that was precisely what she *wanted* to be, *needed* to be—somebody's time-clock puncher!

A sense of confusion, a puzzling lightheadedness swam over her. It was just because she was hungry, she thought, so hungry her stomach was sending up a frantic prayer for deliverance. Let him take her to lunch if he wanted to! She didn't necessarily have to commit herself to anything.

"Well," she murmured, "well, if that's the case, Mr. Reynolds, I don't mind discussing it."

And then she found herself walking dazedly beside him into the green, dark, forestlike interior of The Fernery. At a round white wicker table facing a huge glistening bar, she listened as the man opposite her matter-of-factly described a job that seemed as if it had been stamped out to her precise measurements and embroidered with her initials.

"Yes, luckily I *do* have a passport," she heard herself murmur as they went over the details of the job, and she tried to tell herself that it was real, what was happening, but she didn't really believe it. Didn't believe that she was sitting in that smart room with its hanging baskets of ferns and its white napery and its sterling place settings with masses of blue and purple violets on every table. Didn't believe that she was eating crêpes as delicate as lace and sipping something that made her feel jubilantly alive and that this unexpected, sparkling opportunity lay right there in her lap.

It had turned out to be her lucky day, after all! she thought.

But if that was so, why was this other feeling hovering, this feeling that hit her every time she met Pierce Reynolds' dark, somehow pinioning gaze? Looking at him caused an inexplicable tightening in her. She felt as if she were sinking, sinking . . . as if the waters churning around her were dark, possessive, as if she would have to fight them with all her might or they would snatch her up, sweep her to her doom, and she would be washed away, lost forever.

As Linda had been.

Chapter Three

"You got the notice about the rent increase?" Mrs. Stone's tight, unfriendly face poked out of the door of her apartment. "I guess you're coming to complain, that's what they're all doing."

"Oh, no—it's fine, Mrs. Stone. I've got a job! I'm going to *Vienna!*" Penny said, and just saying the word felt marvelous—how would she feel when she was actually *in* Vienna? For the past two days her heart had been skipping, dancing, doing acrobatics of joy.

"Vienna, huh?" the landlady muttered dubiously and started to close the door.

Penny thrust the big cardboard box with its collection of plants through the opening.

"What's that?" Mrs. Stone stared down at a daffodil bulb as if she thought it might explode.

"My daffodil! And there's a spider plant and some violets. I may not be back for a few weeks, and I was hoping you would keep them. I thought they might cheer you up. Daffodils are really great when you hit a day like this with everything so gloomy and wet."

She was totally unprepared for what happened to the landlady's harshly lined face. Its usual suspicion flared for a second, then quickly gave way to a smile as Mrs. Stone's worn hands tightened around the cardboard box. It was the first smile Penny had even seen from her. Startling how it made the woman look almost . . . almost *sweet*.

"Well, that's very nice of you, Miss Marsh."

"The daffodil should bloom about next week. Bye, Mrs. Stone!" Penny waved as she turned to go back to her apartment.

"Good-bye. Have a good time, Miss Marsh."

Humming the *Blue Danube Waltz,* Penny took the stairs two at a time. Everybody had a soft spot somewhere, she thought, all you had to do was take the trouble to find it. You had to go out of your way to show some interest in people. If you didn't you ended up alone, and what a miserable life *that* was, as she had discovered in these last three dreary months.

And now what she had to do was apply the same philosophy to her dealings with Pierce Reynolds. She was going to show some interest in the man, make him a real friend, someone she would not only work for, but get to know, get to enjoy knowing. It was obvious she needed new human contacts, or else why would she find herself thinking so often about that long lunch at The Fernery? It was simply that she'd been lonely, terribly in need of the stimulation of being with someone, anyone.

The truth was, she had been terribly unfair to

Pierce Reynolds. Allowing the gossip magazines to affect her, influence her feelings. And equating him with a completely different individual, the man Linda had dated.

Beginning with this evening, when she was slated to have dinner with her new employer, she promised herself to look at the man with open eyes, try to see him as himself alone.

Because all those preconceived notions of hers were obviously what lay behind her too-vivid, too-emotional response to the man, once she started to play fair, she might find that Pierce Reynolds was a rather nice person. Now that she looked back on that day at The Fernery, she remembered that his smile had been a warm and spontaneous one and, at times, even admiring. Of course, the admiration had undoubtedly been for her sense of humor—she'd made him laugh several times—rather than for any physical attribute. She was well aware that she was what people called pretty, an innocuous quality, to say the least. She'd never burn up the world with her glamour.

Besides, what really counted to Pierce Reynolds, *and* to herself, was her ability to handle the assignment. If she were successful, he'd even hinted there might be other such assignments, in other parts of the world.

She felt a knot of worry forming between her eyebrows. Was the job as simple as it sounded? All she had to do was fly to Vienna and buy a Guarneri violin from a man named Muller?

"Well, actually, there's a *little* more to it than

that," her new boss had said. "This Muller is somewhat eccentric, not the easiest character to deal with. But, never mind, I'll give you a more thorough briefing . . . let's see, we'll make it Friday over dinner. I'll have all the details worked out by then, but, roughly, I think you can plan on leaving in a week." He sighed. "I wish the destination were Paris. April gives me this terrible yearning to be lolling in a sidewalk café, watching the world go by." His face had held a reminiscent excitement—was he remembering some beautiful girl who had lolled beside him, sipped wine, made promises with her eyes?

He's right, Penny thought, *I am a silly romantic.*

But at the moment how could she be anything else? Here it was, Friday, at last! Tonight he'd give her her plane tickets, "in case we get separated or—and this is always possible—at the last moment I have to back out, leave it all up to you," and her great adventure would be underway! Perfectly natural to have little rills of excitement sweeping up and down her spine. Perfectly natural to wish the hands of the clock would hurry up and announce that it was eight o'clock!

Well, she'd given her plants a home, what else was left to do? Penny looked around the apartment, which somehow seemed drearier than usual. Already her suitcase was piled high with the best pieces left from her college wardrobe which were luckily all classic, lasting things.

Still hanging in her closet were her two best

winter dresses, and now she really had to make a decision, select one most suitable for her dinner tonight with Pierce Reynolds.

Why fuss? she asked herself, *he wouldn't care if you arrived in a grocery bag.*

But just the same she stood for a long time frowning at the dresses. Finally she reached for the lavender wool. Simple in line, softly flared, a completely ladylike dress, and certainly flattering.

And yet . . . the black silk actually excited her, made her feel immensely desirable. Such a pretty oval neckline that showed just the top of her white breasts, cap sleeves that flirted around the roundness of her arms. The black dress would make her look more like the kind of woman Pierce Reynolds would find attractive.

Ridiculous, immature thought! What *was* the matter with her? Had her long spell of living alone and feeling depressed turned her into a vacuous daydreamer, utterly divorced from reality?

Yanking the lavender wool off its hanger, she tossed it on the bed and headed for the shower. She was soaping herself when the telephone rang.

"Oh, darn!"

Snatching a towel, she sprinted, then panted "Yes?" into the receiver.

"Hello, hope I'm not getting you at an inconvenient time."

Catching her half covered, pearly and sopping reflection in the dresser mirror, Penny felt a wave of heat along her damp skin, felt her nipples sharpen shamefully. "Oh, no . . . no . . ."

"Something's come up and I'll have to cancel dinner."

"Oh?" She blinked and all the lights in the world flickered and died. Had he changed his mind? Was it all off—was the wonderful dream about to fade?

"Something big has come up," Pierce Reynolds said crisply. "I'll be on the phone to Paris off and on all evening."

"Perfectly all right," Penny managed.

"But, listen, stay right where you are. I'll get back to you before midnight."

She stared at the phone. *Stay right where you are!* Was he allergic to the word please? Did he expect her to sit waiting for five hours playing tic-tac-toe until he got around to phoning?

"Hello? Miss Marsh? You there?"

"Yes," she said stiffly. "At the moment."

"Right. I'll be in touch as soon as I can get things straightened out on this end, that's a promise."

He hung up, and Penny slammed the receiver down. Huddling in the damp towel she sank on the edge of the bed. He hadn't even bothered with explanations! This had to be the most highhanded character she'd ever encountered. Glumly she stood up, swept the lavender wool back to the closet.

Then all at once she was angrily ripping the black silk from its hanger and slipping into her black bra and panties, her lacy slip, clocked "formal occasion" stockings and her black sling-back pumps.

She'd prepped herself for an evening out, and she was going to have it! Even if the rain ruined her shoes and her hair, she was going to take herself over to her favorite restaurant on Smedley Street. She was going to order shrimp scampi and a glass of white wine and pay for it with the money Pierce Reynolds had given her to handle her preflight expenses. It was only fair, since he'd promised her dinner! And if one of the attractive men who always seemed to be sitting in the bar of that restaurant sent a smile her way, she'd smile right back! She'd been lonely too long. She wasn't going to allow herself one more disappointment! And if Pierce Reynolds phoned and she wasn't in, wasn't there to jump through his hoop, that would just be his hard luck! Priming her for a good time, then expecting her to sit waiting at the phone all night! The gall, the absolute, out-of-this-world gall!

Besides, she suspected this change in plans might mean tomorrow would find her jobless again. She might as well get a little enjoyment while she could!

She blinked, looking around the room. She'd been so terribly eager—so foolish—packing far in advance, giving away her plants!

Forget it; concentrate on now, she told herself sternly.

Half an hour later, sitting in the pink-walled restaurant, sipping her iced Chablis, she found she wasn't enjoying herself after all. The food was delicious, some attractive males at the bar had turned to view her with open admiration—the provocative black silk did set off her shining white-gold hair. But for some reason she wasn't able to indulge in even a little mild flirtation.

Her private celebration had turned sour almost as soon as she sat down at the table because the thought had struck her—even if the assignment was still on, would she be *able* to work with Pierce Reynolds? A man who snapped his fingers and expected her to sit up and beg?

Penny tried to linger over her dessert of Brie and crackers, but she was conscious of the hovering waitress, and looking at the clock she realized she'd stretched the dinner hour far past normal limits, not wanting to go back to the apartment.

I hope he's phoned and phoned. I hope he's finding it all very inconvenient. I hope he realizes I'm nobody's lap dog.

The rain had stopped and overhead the moon looked sharp and clean, as if it, too, had just had a shower.

Penny turned the key in her door, disappointed not to hear her phone clamoring.

Maybe I've cooked my goose. Maybe he'll never call again.

And maybe it was just as well. Maybe they were two people who were basically incompatible and he had realized it.

But the lump of disappointment in her throat wouldn't dissolve. She stared at herself in the mirror. *I don't seduce infants.* . . . But at the moment she didn't look at all childish. The black dress hugged her slender curves the way a lover might.

She looked like a woman yearning for something—for *life*.

And then, somewhere in her consciousness, another thought flared: *Yearning for love?*

Sighing, she undressed and snuggled under the blanket.

She was halfway into an uneasy sleep when the phone shrieked. She heaved up, heart pounding.

And then she forced herself to sit still and stiff, deliberately letting the thing yelp its head off.

On the fifth ring she picked up the receiver. "Hello?"

"Miss Marsh? Say, I'm terribly sorry to be this late. I meant to get back to you sooner, but things piled up like expressway traffic. Afraid I have some unexpected developments, just hope you can go along with them."

Here it goes, Vienna sliding out of my grasp, Penny thought sickly.

"I hope this won't greatly inconvenience you," Pierce Reynolds said. "But you will need to be packed and ready to depart Philadelphia tomorrow afternoon instead of next week. And I'm afraid I'll be going only part of the way with you." He was quiet for a moment and then when she made no response added, "Please say you're not going to back out, I believe you can be of valuable service to me, Miss Marsh."

Chapter Four

"Paris!" Penny cried. "I thought it was Vienna we were going to!"

Pierce Reynolds waved an impatient hand. "I'll straighten it all out when we get to our seats."

A uniformed airport employee tapped Penny's shoulder. "Miss, place your handbag on the conveyor belt, please."

"What?" Penny said confusedly. "Why do I have to do that?"

"So our camera can register its contents and we can make sure you are not carrying a weapon aboard," the man said, and Penny caught Pierce Reynolds' stare. "Haven't you flown before?" he murmured, his dark eyes strangely sympathetic.

She felt herself flushing. "Actually, no—I went to London when I was ten. You know, with my folks, but that was on an ocean liner. I never had occasion to take long trips, college was near enough to drive."

"I see."

She moved alongside him, feeling foolish, set

apart from all the capable-looking career girls striding through the airport. They looked as if they had been *born* on a 747! He must think she was terribly gauche, not even recognizing a metal detector. From now on she'd have to watch everything he did and simply follow suit.

But in a minute her sense of excitement drowned the downbeat feelings—life was a pinwheel, moving so fast it blurred. After his late telephone call, she'd slept only fitfully, rising before dawn to finish all her chores: cleaning out her refrigerator, remembering to leave bird food on her window ledge, writing to Linda's folks, doing her nails, returning library books. Remembering what she'd read about jet lag, she tried to take a nap, but her pounding heart made that impossible.

It was midafternoon when Pierce Reynolds' chauffeur-driven limo had pulled up at Mrs. Stone's weather-beaten front door. In moments Penny found herself propelled into an atmosphere of pure luxury. Pierce Reynolds' chauffeur had carried out her suitcase, poured coffee for her from the electric pot that stood near the champagne and liquor supply on the car's bar and then Pierce Reynolds, after explaining tersely that they were driving to New York to catch the evening flight out of JFK, passed her a small raffia tray that sat on the seat between them. A pale green dish, shaped like an avacado, held a shrimp salad. Iced grapes and a selection of pink and white bon bons nestled alongside two tiny sweet rolls. "Tide you over to dinner," her new employer said. But she was too breathless to take more than a few nibbles.

During the two-and-a-half-hour car ride, the man beside her didn't address her again. He spent every minute reading complicated papers and barking orders into a recorder.

And now here they were, boarding the giant silver jet, and still not a word of explanation about the change in destination.

Oh, well, why quibble about Paris? Penny thought, as she struggled to keep up with her boss's long strides. It was fascinating, she thought, how much like a living room the first class section was, the chairs so deep and comfortable, so much elbow room, generous-size tables.

"I took care to get you a window seat," Pierce Reynolds said, and flashed a smile. Now that he had finished with his countless papers and turned them over to his chauffeur to give to his secretary, he was much more relaxed. Certainly a striking looking man, Penny thought. She loved the suit he was wearing, a pale beige hopsacking with a hint of gold in the material. Had he selected it to play up the gold sparks in his thick brown hair? Or perhaps, with a wardrobe so exquisitely coordinated, he had a woman around to help him?

Like an echo of the thought, the willowy redheaded stewardess drew up alongside his chair. Smiling in an intimate way, showing more dimples than should be allowed by law, the girl murmured, "So nice to see *you* again, Mr. Reynolds. It's been too long."

"Much too long, Dotty. Getting yourself a stopover in Paris this trip?"

The girl's eyes had a mischievous look. "Now that you're aboard, I wish I could say yes, but I have to head right back. You want your usual champagne?" She looked briefly at Penny. "Champagne, Miss?"

"I think not for the lady, she's new to flying."

Penny stiffened. "But *not* to champagne, Mr. Reynolds. Yes, thank you, I will have a glass."

As the stewardess moved off, Pierce Reynolds said in a low voice, "Say, sorry I embarrassed you, I just didn't want you feeling repercussions. Sometimes on a first flight . . ."

"I can make such decisions myself, Mr. Reynolds, I *am* over twenty-one!" She certainly wasn't going to tell him she'd had champagne only once before in her life.

"Sorry. I guess from my neck of the woods—I'm thirty-three—you look like a . . . if you can bear the pun . . . a very new penny."

She wouldn't let herself smile; she was feeling an inexplicable need to scratch at him. "Would you please tell me why we're going to Paris? I told everybody my destination was Vienna. I don't particularly like the idea that nobody in the world will know where I am."

"You mean you might be in the hands of a white slaver? Abducted and held captive in some faraway den of iniquity?"

"You may laugh if you want, it *has* been known to happen! But I can guarantee you if anyone abducted me, he'd have a fight on his hands. I'm *not* made of jelly!"

His eyes made a quick survey, from her face to her ankles. "Obviously not. But you forget, we white slavers enjoy combative women—they put a little spice in our work. White slavers can get terribly bored." His eyes moved slowly over her, lingering on her lips, her throat, and mocking her every minute.

Face burning, Penny struggled up from her seat. "Mr. Reynolds, this isn't going to work! If you are taking advantage of your position as an employer . . . I'm just going to get off this plane!"

"And live on the great wealth in your funds-on-hand column? What was it, a hundred and fifty-three dollars?"

Penny let out a furious breath. "That's *my* business! You can't seem to understand that I'm not at all interested in any . . . after-hours activities with you! Not every girl in the world is impressed by wealth and power, you know. Some of us still have standards!"

"Wealth and power . . . is that the sum total of my appeal?" He smiled in an odd way. "Sit down."

"Pardon me?"

"You know I've given you the ideal job! So sit down. You can't get off now anyway. As for your precious standards, no one's going to pry you loose from them." His hand shot out and

clamped around her wrist. "Sit down, I promise
to ease all your doubts and fears. Paris is *my*
destination, you're going on to Vienna."

Penny pulled her wrist away, but it was plain
she had made her point, so she sank slowly back
in her seat. The spot on her wrist where he had
held it felt as hot as if it had been burned.

"I'll start with the phone call I got yesterday."
He studied his handsome Swiss shoes. "That
was what led to my having to cancel our dinner
plans. My most reliable Paris representative was
calling about a possible . . ." his voice turned to
a whisper, "a possible Manet found in an art
shop. Unsigned. My contact couldn't be sure if it
was just a copy or the real thing, then had a
feeling it *was* real, hurried back to buy it for me
and someone else had snagged it! What I'm
going to do, of course, is try to track it down. A
rough job, but naturally it would be an absolutely priceless acquisition, and it's in fine condition."

"What has all this to do with me . . . my job in
Vienna?"

"Nothing actually, you can make your Vienna
connection as soon as we reach Paris. But flying
together gives me the opportunity to talk to you
about your assignment."

"I see." Penny felt somewhat mollified, and
was distressed to realize that the stewardess'
dimpling smiles at him had been responsible for
a good part of her annoyance. It was a reaction
she'd have to analyze later, when she was alone.

"Mr. Reynolds, you also said you'd tell me more about this man who owns the violin."

"And so I will. But look—since we're going to be traveling together for quite a stretch, I have a proposition. Now, wait a minute—don't raise your eyebrows that way—what I'm proposing is a truce. It would make both of us a lot more comfortable."

She looked at him. His eyes met hers levelly, with no sign of the mockery she was growing to expect.

"In fact, with a little extra effort," he went on wryly, "we might even get to enjoy each other's company. How do you vote?"

"Well, I've always been on the side of civilized behavior."

"For starters, let's get down to first names. That might melt some of the barbs on the wire. Penny and Pierce. Say, it's a rather euphonious combination. Sounds like an old vaudeville team, doesn't it?"

At which point he gave her an absolutely devastating smile, showing gleaming, perfectly shaped teeth and Penny felt herself start to blush. It was as if someone had dipped a brush into a huge paint pot and was coloring every inch of her in tones of rose.

Luckily, the stewardess' voice over the intercom diverted their attention, or at least Penny's, apparently the safety spiel was familiar stuff to the other passengers. But she was grateful for the interruption. It took her mind off the man sitting so close to her. Why couldn't she really relax with him? Why did she always have this on-the-brink feeling? Every time he looked at her, she felt so awkward, as if her lipstick must be smudged or her slip hanging down.

And now the giant jet was lifting its nose, shooting straight up, silver wings glinting in the brilliant light from the dying sun.

"It's so incredibly *smooth!*" Penny cried.

Pierce Reynolds looked amused. "It's the landing that's a little hair-raising for the first time flyer."

"I don't think I'll mind in the least! This is really enjoyable."

"Look out your window and see what's become of mighty New York."

She obeyed, then clapped a hand over her mouth in astonished delight. "Oh, it's so small, like a toy village!"

There was a small silence. Then he said in a low voice, "You have a marvelous quality of wonder."

Smiling, she turned to him. "What do you mean?"

But before he could answer, a strong perfume and a presence wafted around them. "Here I am, back again!"

It was the dimpled stewardess, working the dimples as if each one were paid time and a half. Penny felt an odd sense of triumph as Pierce, reaching for the champagne, gave Dotty Dimples barely a glance.

When the stewardess had dejectedly drifted

away, Penny said, "Another thing I'd like you to clarify, Mr. Reynolds . . ."

"Pierce."

"*Pierce*. I can't understand why you need *me*. I mean, since you're going to Europe anyway, why couldn't *you* buy this violin?"

"I knew you'd get around to asking that. Well, several reasons—the main one being because I am who I am and you are what you are." He drew a small leather notebook out of his briefcase. "Look," his finger stabbed at the page of boldly written notes, "I made this notation two years ago, when I first found out this Muller owned a Guarneri. See what I wrote? *Figure out how to approach owner*. Then, when I ran into you, I was sure I had the answer to how to approach him."

"I'm more puzzled than ever."

"All right, let me put this question to you. As a violin lover, how would you feel about a chance to play a Guiseppe Guarneri?"

"Oh!" Penny gasped. "It would be . . . it would thrill me to death! It would be like a dream!"

His eyes moved over her face, and he sat back, smiling as if enormously pleased about something. "Well, then, Penny, you're going to have a dream come true. And our Mr. Muller is going to be one completely smitten man. He'll never be able to resist you."

Penny shook her head. "Maybe I'm slow, but . . ."

"Look, Muller has never shown any inclination to part with this instrument."

"I understand that! A Guarneri is second only to a Strad. I mean, there are only a few hundred in existence!"

"Yes, and this particular violin is a family heirloom. One of the Mullers was a violinist back in the eighteenth century. Muller himself doesn't play, he's a biochemist, but he loves music. Which will make you absolutely irresistible. Once he sees you, innocent, big eyed, in all your spiritual beauty—once you play his instrument—well, that's when he'll be willing to sell, if he ever will."

"That's very flattering, but . . ."

His face sharpened. "I never flatter, not when it comes to a business deal. Just judging from what I know of Muller my information leads me to conclude that he'd never go for the crass commercial approach of a deal. And I certainly don't want other dealers getting into the act, putting bids in against me. Which is why I need your services."

"But what makes you think he'll sell at *all*, if he's never wanted to before this?"

"That's something else again. Through my contacts, I have a connection with someone who knows Muller slightly. This source has fed me some information about the man." He looked at her with a deep gaze that made her throat go dry. "You see, according to my informant, this Muller, this scholarly middle-aged gentleman, has been swept away by passion. He's been seen around Vienna with a gorgeous young thing who drives a gorgeous sports car—the kind of lush beauty who wants expensive things and plenty of them. So this is the time in Mr. Muller's life when he could use extra cash, the time when he may be motivated to neglect old sentiments for . . . shall we say more immediate pleasures?"

"I see."

"Of course, I can't say this information is absolutely reliable. But I do think if Muller ever sells, he'll sell to someone he knows will cherish that violin. Someone like you. And another plus is, he'll recognize and respect your father's name—did he ever play in Vienna?"

"I don't think so. I believe he played in Munich once."

"Good enough. When you talk to Muller, you can bring that out, that'll sit well. Everything about you will sit well with him."

"Thank you," Penny murmured, quickly swallowing some champagne.

"Don't thank me—thank whoever gave you the prize genes that add up to Aegean Sea eyes and naturally gold hair. Now, I'm not getting personal—only a fool would deny that beauty is a plus for any woman."

Penny felt the blush starting again, washing her with rosiness. Luckily he didn't seem to notice. He *was* being impersonal. The compliment had been pronounced as matter-of-factly as if it were a stock market quotation.

"Actually," he went on, "the man will be getting a very good price if he sells to us. I have no intention of cheating him, you know. But I do

want to avoid competitive bidding. In this in-
flated economy, that can get really rough." He
leaned across her to point to the window. "The
Big Apple is nothing but a snow bank."

Penny gazed at the white vaporish world
around them. "It's like fairyland!" Turning to
look back at her companion, she saw he hadn't
been looking at the view. What was he thinking,
staring at her that way? Quickly she reached for
her glass again, and took a generous swallow.
Instantly she felt easier, much more like herself.
"I don't really approve of you, you know," she
said daringly, and yet half playfully.

"Mademoiselle, you have given me vague inti-
mations to that effect." His lips smiled, but his
eyes were watchful. "But we *have* declared a
truce, haven't we?"

"I just have to say I don't approve of anybody
who treats musical instruments like merchandise! I guess that makes *me* a hypocrite, doesn't
it? I mean, to take a job like this?"

"Perhaps you're not aware we investment people take better care of instruments than some
musicians. I've seen them put a priceless instrument on the edge of a table where it could crash
to the floor in a minute."

"Well, that's true. Dad was careful, but some
aren't. It's just that I absolutely cringe at the
idea of locking a violin away in a vault . . .
burying its voice."

"An air-conditioned vault keeps that voice in
top form."

"But a violin's made to be *played!*"

"I hire people to keep my instruments tuned up." He reached across the chair arm and Penny started as he took her hand in his.

"What . . . ?" The wine had made her reactions a little slow.

He was still holding her fingers, studying them. "Yes, you have an artistic, nimble hand. Will you play for me when we get the Guarneri?"

"*If* we get it," Penny said shakily, "of course."

"I'll look forward to the experience."

"Oh, really, I'm not that good, it's nothing!" She drew her hand away. And then she sat stiffly looking down at it. It felt odd, tingly. It was the same sensation she'd felt when he'd clasped her wrist.

"May I have some more champagne?" she said scratchily.

He gave her a quick look, but in a few minutes another bubbly glass was at her elbow. While she sipped, he pointed out that he knew nothing about the condition of Muller's violin, "it might not even be playable, that's why I need somebody who can tell by drawing a bow over it." Then he went on to talk about his start in the investment business. "Actually at the tender age of eight, my grass cutting earnings went into stamp collecting. I specialized in Vatican City stamps and luckily they went sky-high in value. When I needed college money, my collection paid the tuition."

Telling her how poor his family had been, his heavily lashed eyes took on a steeliness. He'd never had a room of his own, or a bicycle or even a baseball mitt. And his first Christmas tree was one he found in the gutter.

"It still had shreds of tinsel hanging from it. I thought it was beautiful. I remember lugging it up three flights of stairs to our kitchen. *I've got a tree for us!* I told my mother. I couldn't understand why she cried, I expected her to be happy. I didn't know there was anything pitiable about putting up a tree when Christmas had been *over* for a week!"

Looking at him, Penny felt a strange tightness in her throat. She had to fight a sudden driving impulse to reach out and smooth the faint horizontal lines in his forehead. She could see the little boy with the Christmas tree so clearly. And see how such a boy, yearning and deprived, could grow into an ambitious, ever striving man.

"I guess you have a super Christmas tree now."

He smiled. "I have, without a doubt, the most stunning tree in the city of Philadelphia. In fact, I don't mind telling you my trim-the-tree parties have a certain cachet. You'll have to come see for yourself."

She didn't answer, and he leaned closer. "Will you?" He gazed at her, the pupils of his eyes very big and dark, his lips slightly parted.

She looked away in a hurry. "Of course!" She made her voice very bright and brittle. "Being invited to trim the tree has it all over coming to see your etchings! Although I suppose you've got women a block long—since your parties have such cachet!"

As soon as the silly words were out, she regretted them. What *was* the matter with her? There had been no reason at all to talk like that. It had been downright rude, and certainly not anything an employee should say!

"No, not a whole block." Pierce's voice was frosty. "Just half a block—but we're working on a bigger crowd for this year." Obviously nettled, he picked up a magazine and started flipping through its bright pages.

Penny sank back in her chair. He had every right to be annoyed, she thought, biting her lip. Downing the rest of the champagne, she fixed her eyes on the swirling cloud banks that looked the way she had always pictured heaven. Why was she snapping at this man, nipping at his heels? It was so senseless. Here he'd given her an exciting job at a more than satisfactory salary, and she was handing out nothing but unpleasantness.

She closed her eyes, feeling miserable and self-conscious, and all at once terribly tired. In fact, she had the feeling she'd never be able to unglue her eyelids again. Oh, it had been *such* a long night, *such* an exciting day and this bubbly champagne was so good and this was a very comfortable seat, soft and warm, like having someone's arms around you. *Were* someone's arms around her? Something seemed to be touching her, caressing her shoulders, but she couldn't raise her eyelids . . . simply couldn't . . . such terribly heavy weights . . . just couldn't look at anything. . . .

When she woke she was conscious of three things: the soft cashmere scarf that someone had draped around her shoulders, the wonderful odor of charcoal-grilled steak and the man looking down at her with an unreadable expression in his eyes.

"Oh! *Oh!*" She blinked her fogged eyes. "Where *are* we? How long have I been sleeping? Is this your scarf?"

He laughed. "May I take those in order? One, we're now over the Atlantic Ocean. Two, you've had a typical champagne-induced nap, quite a good one. And yes, that is my scarf."

"Oh, oh, I must look terrible! Where do you—?"

"You don't look terrible. You simply look like any infant after a healthy sleep. And the room you require is right down the aisle."

She flushed. "Well, if you'll excuse me . . ."

The red-headed stewardess was emerging from the lavatory as Penny arrived. Dotty cast a quick, critical look in her direction and Penny could see why when she looked in the mirror. Hair terribly messed, lipstick nonexistent, mascara smudged.

He'd been looking at her, seeing her like this. What had he thought, staring in that concentrated way? That she was a mess, or could he perhaps be wondering if she were . . . conquerable? After all, a girl far away from all strictures of home . . . And certainly he didn't seem like a man who cultivated celibacy.

Quickly she powdered the flush away from her face and made sundry other improvements. And then, without warning, the thought gripped her: *If I ever gave myself to anyone, it would be to that man.*

Erase that thought, she ordered her consciousness.

When she found the man for her, he would be gentle, thoughtful. Not a sometime man—a forever man.

She was being swept away by the sudden excitement of her life, she told herself, not by Pierce Reynolds.

A tall man in a pilot's uniform was strolling in the aisle as she emerged from the powder room. He glanced at her and then glanced again. "Enjoying your trip?" he said pleasantly.

"Oh, yes! Are you—well, you *can't* be our pilot!" She laughed uncertainly. "Or else we'd be falling down!"

His laugh joined hers. He had uneven features, but a very appealing expression in his gray eyes. "I'm a pilot, but at the moment I'm getting a few days of R and R, spending them in the City of Light, of course. You staying in Paris?"

"I wish I were!"

"I do, too. I'm John Carpenter—could I interest you in some champagne and companionship?"

"Oh, I'm sorry. I'm with someone." Penny motioned to Pierce Reynolds.

At that moment Pierce looked over his shoulder at them. His dark eyebrows shirred, then his eyes went past them, their expression blank.

"Well, have a nice time wherever you're headed." John Carpenter's smile was flatteringly warm. "Hope we run into each other again sometime."

"That would be nice."

When she slipped back into her chair, Pierce was reading his magazine again—rather too intently, Penny thought.

More probably, though, she was reading things into his behavior. Thirty-three years old . . . he'd known a lot of devastating girls by this time—why should he have any thoughts at all about her? Suddenly she was miserably conscious of the worn look of her camel hair suit, and the slightly faded pale blue cashmere sweater that had seen her through four years of college and was ready to be graduated to the trash bin.

"Someday I'm going to spend time in Paris. I'm going to see the Arc de Triomphe and I'm going to buy a Paris gown!" she was speaking half to herself and half to her employer.

"The Arc de Triomphe and a Paris gown—that's an interesting combination—I approve." Smiling, he put his magazine aside. "Run into a friend?" He inclined his head to the aisle where she'd been standing with John Carpenter.

"Just a friendly airline employee, promoting good will among the customers." She added impishly: "The way the stewardess was promoting good will with you."

He looked at her and suddenly threw his head back and laughed. It was such a contagious sound that Penny followed suit, and in the next hour, as they were served their steak dinners, there was quite a lot of laughing. Somehow they fell into a silly game, trying to find faces in the whirling clouds outside the window. "See that long shape over there? That's Jimmy Durante—there's his nose!" Pierce said. "I see someone with a beard—it's Father Time!" Penny cried. It was all light and easy, and when they had finished dessert they enjoyed the evening's movie, which had a Parisian setting. "This just whets my appetite to see Paris for myself," Penny whispered. "Well, if you're going to work for me, you'll be duty bound to see it often," Pierce said, "and if I'm lucky, I'll get some free time occasionally and be your tour guide."

That sounded very promising, Penny thought; perhaps they were really learning to relax with each other, perhaps now there would be no more unsettling undercurrents, unnatural blushes or ridiculous quickened heartbeats.

Together they watched night spread its velvety wings around the plane and together, while the great Atlantic rolled silently, distantly, beneath them, they drifted into sleep.

Morning lay pale against the window when Penny opened her eyes and once again met Pierce's quick smile. He looked thoroughly awake and as immaculately groomed as when he had boarded the plane. "We'll be in Paris in time for breakfast croissants," he said. "Then we'll put you on your plane for Vienna and I'll join you when my business is finished." He looked at his watch. "Right on the button, I'm happy to say. My Paris representative will be waiting for me."

"Won't you have even a minute for fun? Will you work every second you're there?"

"Oh, I'll manage a little relaxation—I told you I love Paris."

"That's nice." She was sorry she'd brought it up—it was too easy to imagine what he meant by relaxation. "I wish I knew German," she said. "You think I'll have any trouble in Vienna? I'll have to use my phrasebook a lot."

He smiled. "Girls with eyes like yours somehow get their message across in any language. And, as I told you, Muller has lived in America, fortunately."

"I can manage the 'please and thank you' kind of thing in German, and, of course, I know college French. Everybody in Europe speaks French, don't they?"

"Don't sound so anxious. It'll be all right. Besides, I'll be on hand to keep you out of trouble as soon as I find out what gives with this Manet." He nodded toward the window. "Getting close. Watch for a long stretch of gray-green stone with a satin ribbon winding down the middle. The ribbon is the Seine and Paris lies on either side. But wait, maybe you'd better *not* look—first landings can be something of a shock."

"Oh, I'll be fine. You've turned me into a flying bug!"

"Here, put this in your mouth right away."

She looked down at the chewing gum.

"Go on, take it. When we start down, chew hard." He pushed it at her. "Well, come on."

Still she said nothing, studying the pulsing nerve in his cheek.

"Will you come to life? I told you we're going down, your ears are going to feel the drop in pressure."

"I don't want any gum."

"Why not? Don't you like the flavor?"

"I don't like the arrogance. You sound as if you're talking to a galley slave."

His eyes flashed for a moment. Then he shrugged. "Do as you please. Be uncomfortable and ridiculous if you enjoy it."

"Now, Mr. Reynolds," the chiding yet flirtatious voice belonged to Dotty Dimples, back again, leaning her ample bosom over Pierce, "don't you be mean to the ladies, a handsome fellow like you!" Smiling knowingly, the stewardess then directed some advice to Penny. "Keep him away from the Folies. We stewardesses know we always run second to his French chorus girls."

Penny, turning to look at Pierce, saw that the remark actually seemed to please him! *What an ego*, she thought tightly.

And yet, as Dotty swayed on down the aisle, she heard herself say, too thinly, "Are they fun—the French chorus girls?"

But her voice was drowned by the voice over the intercom: "Ladies and gentlemen, we are beginning our descent into Paris and it looks like a lovely spring morning. We hope you will enjoy your stay in the City of Light. And now will you kindly fasten your seat belts."

Penny complied and turned to the window.

The sickening sensation assailed her before she had time to resist it. The billowing clouds were parting and all at once, beneath her, winding roads and steeples and rooftops were visible and rushing up to meet her, growing bigger, closer . . .

There was a sudden, terrifying jolt. "Oh!" she cried, as the jet engines set up a howl. And now she was falling, falling, and there was an uncomfortable hollow feeling in her ears, and she twisted in her seat and saw Pierce turn to stare at her.

And then all at once it wasn't physical discomfort she was feeling . . .

Because at that moment the shattering thought hit her—her parents had met their death in precisely this way, hurtling down, down, the plane splintering into a thousand fragments, the two dearest people in the world scattered like seed in the wind.

The vivid picture was too much to bear; she twisted in her seat, groped for the man beside her. The helpless tears streamed from her, and wouldn't stop. She realized for the first time how spectacularly beautiful life was, and how easily it could be lost forever. *Oh, make me cherish every minute,* she thought, as she felt Pierce's hand close firmly on hers. Tears had blinded her, she couldn't see his face. But she heard his voice, softer than she had ever heard it. "I'm here, I'm right here," he was saying in her ear.

Her tears subsided and she felt a vast emotional weariness. "I'm sorry to be such a mess," she choked. "It's just—you see, my parents were flying to the West Coast to see a doctor—a new treatment for Dad's arthritis—and then . . . it happened. This . . . this just made me think of them . . . *remember* them. They were so . . . so . . ."

His eyes were soft with sympathy. She realized his arm was around her, a strong circle of support. "You're a lovely girl," he whispered.

The blinding joy she felt came so quickly on the heels of her sorrow that it was dizzying, shocking and yet, in a way, completely natural, as if the memory of loss had sharpened her need to have someone in the world to love, someone to love her in return.

But then, gradually, her good sense stirred, and she edged away from the man. He had simply been sympathetic and immediately she had read all kinds of intimacies into that casual feeling. And it was all to the good that he wasn't really interested in her. She certainly didn't want to add her name to his long list of conquests. Chorus girls, stewardesses and one silly ninny who couldn't face up to the facts of life?

I won't soften like that again, won't let myself love him, Penny thought fiercely. *I'll cut the feeling out now, be ruthless.*

Because if I let this fascination flourish, I'll be wasting that gift of life—ruining what I've just pledged to cherish.

Chapter Five

"Where are we *going*?" Penny gasped. "I thought I was supposed to be heading for a plane to Vienna! Didn't you say I had just enough time to make the connection?"

Answering with an impatient gesture, Pierce hurried her across the pavement to the limousine. She caught sight of her dented suitcase being loaded into the trunk, along with his impressive alligator bags. "My luggage! It should be checked in for the flight!"

"Come on, get in." He held the car door for her. She hesitated, then sighed helplessly and slid in. She heard him give the name of a hotel to the driver, and then he was settling in the seat beside her looking at her sternly.

"Did you think I'd be so callous as to ship you off to another plane after the emotional storm you've just gone through?" His voice was almost harsh.

"But I'm all right now! *Really!* I don't usually fly off the handle that way—I apologize!"

"Don't be so hard on yourself. Under the circumstances you have a right to be upset. I don't think you've really quite completed the grieving process."

"Maybe you're right, people kept telling me to let go, cry—but I was too busy, working hard. I was determined to graduate at the top of the class—you know, for *them*. . . ." Penny drew a shaky breath, but managed to keep control. "I shouldn't be burdening you with my personal problems."

"Do I give any indication you're burdening me?" His eyes darkened and he moved slightly away from her. "You know, sometimes I get the distinctly unpleasant feeling you don't like me very much, don't trust me."

"Well, I . . . no . . ." She looked down at her tense hands. How could she explain that even if she learned to trust him, she'd never be able to trust herself in relation to him?

"You don't have to spare my feelings just because I'm the one who signs your paycheck."

"I'd never predicate my reactions on something like that! I just . . . well, I would prefer to keep my feelings completely neutral in relationship to you."

"A very sensible policy," he said stiffly. "I'll do my best to reciprocate."

Penny had to look away quickly or she might simply melt against him, make a fool of herself for the second time in the space of a few hours.

The truth was, she was surprised and shaken that he was so considerate of her needs. She *had* been dreading boarding another plane right away. She needed time to pull herself together.

"The phone call I made at the airport was to the hotel," Pierce said coolly. "Luckily I was able to get you accommodations. I suggest you get plenty of rest and catch up with your jet lag. That way, when you start for Vienna tomorrow, you'll be thoroughly refreshed."

"That's very thoughtful. Thank you."

"I'm just protecting my own interests, keeping you in shape for your assignment."

He turned to look out the window, and she found herself staring hungrily and helplessly at his profile, at the thick fringe of his eyelashes, the soft, glistening, gold-flecked hair. His skin was so smooth and taut and tan. She could imagine the feel of it, satiny, but underneath the fine strong bone structure.

"Perhaps you'll have time to take a taxi to the Arc. You said you were eager to see it. I'd take you myself, but as I told you, Anne Martel, my Paris representative, is meeting me immediately. However, I *would* like all three of us to have dinner together. Anne can teach you quite a lot about investment buying."

So his Paris contact was a woman! Determinedly Penny fixed her attention on the scenery: long windows with graceful sheer curtains, bright flower boxes, and striped awnings went by in a jumble that was almost frightening. Apparently the stories she'd read about reckless French drivers hadn't been exaggerated.

Suddenly the narrow road became a wide,

ruler-straight city boulevard. She pinned her eyes on the panorama of green-and-blue tiled rooftops, monuments majestic against the April sky, palatial mansions and cobblestone streets.

"Oh, all the flowers!" she breathed. "Chestnuts in blossom!"

"Yes, just like the song. They're all along the *Champs Elysées*—for my money, the most magnificent promenade anywhere. Your famous Arc is right at the end of the boulevard." He smiled out at the passing scene. "Paris is a city to fall in love with, a city to fall in love *in*, for that matter."

"Speaking from experience?" she asked lightly.

He darted a look at her. "Did you think I spent every waking hour with the *Wall Street Journal*? Or every sleeping hour, for that matter?"

"Not after meeting Dotty Dimples!"

His white teeth flashed a grin. "That's a good name for her, she *does* look a little like a doll, doesn't she? Those rounded cheeks and saucer eyes."

"She walks, talks, rolls her eyes—the question is, is she real or wax?" The words had popped out before she could recall them. "Ouch! I don't know why I said that. I think maybe I need breakfast."

"I would have been a little more flattered if you'd let the remark stand. It would have been rather rejuvenating . . . thinking I could make someone so young and pretty a little . . . jealous. It would have made my day."

"Sorry, your day will have to stay unmade!" Cheeks hot, she slapped the words out. "I told you, I try to keep personal feelings out of business arrangements."

"If you think back on what you just said, isn't that a little illogical?" His eyes were mocking.

"I don't know what you're talking about!"

And then the driver was pulling up at their hotel, and Pierce was staying behind to supervise the luggage unloading, and there was the welcome flurry of entering the lobby and signing the register and being escorted upstairs by *le chasseur*, the bellboy. And there was the delight of standing in a perfectly beautiful room, windows swathed in yards and yards of gold Scalamandre silk, walls silk-paneled and looking up to see that the ceiling over the Empire bed was completely mirrored.

Whatever for? Penny thought and then found her cheeks on fire. Quickly she lowered her eyes from the mirror and turned to the bellboy. *"Pouvons-nous prendre le petit déjeuner dans la chambre?"* She spoke slowly and prayerfully —she'd never before put her classroom French to the practical test.

"Oui, certainement, Madame."

"Mademoiselle," Penny corrected and saw the bellboy's quick, odd look. But then her attention was diverted. Pierce stood in the doorway, eyebrows puzzling. "I can't figure this—Anne definitely said she would meet me, but there's no sign of her—not even a message at the desk."

"That's too bad." Deliberately she refused to

71

allow her thoughts to linger on the woman he called his "Paris contact."

"Yes. I had hoped to get down to the art gallery, have a talk with the owner. But I don't know *which* gallery she found the painting in and Anne's secretary has no idea where she is. Strange, it's not at all like Anne." He sighed. "Well . . . I overheard you ordering breakfast— mind if I join you? Oh, and by the way, your French isn't at all bad."

"*If* I stick to simple sentences and pronounce them very, very carefully." But it pleased her that he had noticed. Turning to the waiting bellboy, she said: "*Puis-je avoir la carte?*"

As he trotted off to get the menu, Pierce strode across the velvety gold carpet to the window. "You have your own terrace out here." He drew the draperies open. "I've put people up in this room before, it's the loveliest view available."

"Oh! Oh, how breathtaking!" Penny stared down at the courtyard. She had read about Paris's inner courtyards, but had never expected to find anything so lovely—masses of brilliant spring flowers sent up their heady perfume and gaily striped umbrellas billowed over white wrought iron tables. Uniformed waiters stood around, waiting for their breakfast patrons. "Can we eat right here on the balcony?" she said excitedly.

"Of course. And may I suggest caviar with your croissants?"

"For breakfast?"

"Why not? Caviar hasn't a time of day, it's like

champagne—it's for all time. I'm going to have to teach you to think like a woman of the Continent."

"I haven't the slightest objection!" Penny laughed.

The meal was served to them by an elderly waiter so polite he was almost reverent. Penny, dipping into the exquisite little silver pot of caviar, thought, *This isn't a meal—it's a gastronomic adventure.*

And then she looked up and caught Pierce's expression.

He was frowning, looking at his watch.

"What's the matter?"

"Anne—I'm worried about her. I hope she hasn't had an accident; the traffic in this town is insane. But, of course, she's used to it. . . ." His voice trailed off. "It's just so unlike her not to be here, she's the most competent of women. I wonder . . . if that front desk made a stupid error and didn't pass on her message. . . ." He slapped down his napkin. "If that's the case, this place will lose my patronage, I guarantee you! Carelessness and sloppiness on the job are inexcusable!"

His flushed face showed how upset he was. Unreasonably so, Penny thought, since he wasn't at all sure there had *been* any message in the first place.

"Oh, I'm sure you'll hear soon," she murmured placatingly. "Just allow her a little leeway."

"A little leeway! She's almost an hour late!"

"But so many things could have delayed her. She could have had a flat tire or maybe she just overslept. After all, people aren't programmed like computers."

"Oh, now I'm in for a little philosophical discourse on human nature?" He stood up abruptly, his glance withering.

Penny looked indignantly at him. "No—I would never presume to do anything like that! I'm sure you know all there is to know on that subject, and every other subject in the book!" Her voice was sharper than she had meant it to be for suddenly, seeing the arrogant set of his mouth, she had found herself remembering Linda's lover—how, time after time, despite the requests and protests of the campus police, he had run his Mercedes up on the quad's grass rather than use the parking area ordinary people were restricted to. Men like that could never be told anything, she thought sourly, they knew all the answers and ignored the rules average people obeyed.

And then another thought occurred: Was he emotionally involved with this "Paris contact" of his? Certainly he seemed disproportionately worried about the woman's lateness. . . .

Sitting stiffly at her place, unable to go on with her meal, she watched Pierce Reynolds leave the balcony and pluck up the telephone on her night table. From the ensuing conversation, it was obvious that there had not been any messages from Anne. He dropped the phone annoyedly, then picked it up again, and in a moment he was asking questions in rapid French. When he hung up, his face wore a relieved expression. "That was Anne's secretary. She's been held up," he called to Penny. "But she'll definitely meet us here for dinner."

"That's good," Penny said distantly. She left the balcony and moved slowly into the room.

"All right." His voice was brusque. "You're free now to catch up with your rest. I'll see you this evening at six, in the main dining room."

He swung away from her, stalking not to the door but to the closets.

"Where are you *going*?" she said after him.

The mirrored closets were in a wall-to-wall row. Palming the knob on the last one, he said tersely: "We connect here," and flung the door open.

It didn't lead to a closet at all! Their rooms were joined!

She had naturally assumed he was somewhere down the hall, had never imagined only a door separated them! What had he said, "I've put people up in this room before." *People*? Meaning his women? And the bellboy calling her Madame—giving her that odd look. . . . Because he remembered other women who had been in this room—women who had perhaps registered as Madame Reynolds? It wouldn't surprise her in the least.

"Mr. Reynolds," she heard the high strained sound of her voice, "Mr. Reynolds, I don't care much for this kind of arrangement."

He turned, stared darkly. "*What* kind of arrangement? Something about the room you don't like?"

"No, not the room, the *door*—that connecting door!"

"And what, may I ask, is your objection?"

"The same one most women would have. People could get a very wrong idea."

"Oh . . . and what idea is that?" There was an odd shine to his eyes. "Tell me about it."

"It's obvious, isn't it? And it's . . . it's very unfair! I'm an employee, nothing more. I wouldn't want anyone, your friend who's coming tonight or even the bellboy, to get the idea there was something . . . intimate . . . going on here."

He looked almost as if he were going to laugh. Then he turned and walked back to where she was standing. For a long moment he looked steadily down into her eyes, and Penny felt her knees melting, her bones slowly turning to butter.

"I don't see anything horrifying about an idea like that," he said in a low voice.

She wasn't ready for what followed—wasn't ready for the strong arms that captured her, the hard firm body that moved so possessively against hers, and felt so vividly, urgently male. *"Please!"* she gasped. His face stared into hers and a thundering sound filled her ears—her own heartbeats—and then his mouth covered hers in a burning, piratical kiss, and for a moment she felt a surge of response that startled and rocked her, sent shivers of delight and shame up and down the length of her body. *"Please!"* she managed to gasp, pulling away and moving backward.

Her fingers closed on the edge of the night table. Using its solidity to steady herself, she took another backward step.

She felt something snag her heel. *"Oh!"* Suddenly she was toppling sideways, sinking onto the bed, the satin spread slithering and sliding under her.

And Pierce Reynolds was moving closer, bending over her, a kind of savage smile on his face, his intent plain in his eyes.

"No!" she cried. "Don't you dare touch me!"

He hung over her for a long moment, as if half doubting her sincerity. "You're sure about that, little girl?"

"As sure as I'm breathing!" Penny cried.

He sat back slowly, the pulse in his throat throbbing like something captured, but when he spoke again his voice was silky. "I think we look rather well together," he gestured toward the ceiling mirror, "the nymph and the satyr."

Penny's cheeks burned as she saw the reflection, their bodies so close on the satin-sheathed bed.

We look rather well together . . . yes, her fairness and his dark suntanned looks perfectly complemented each other. In the mirror they had looked like young lovers on the very brink of fulfillment. . . .

What would it feel like to lie in his arms, close as close could be to this man with the mocking, heart-stopping smile?

Angry at him and at her own too vivid thoughts, Penny pushed herself up from the bed. "Is *this* why you hire girls to travel with you?" she rasped. "Is this the real reason you gave me a job? My pay is Vienna . . . and *you*?"

The words found their target. He rose slowly, his face pale beneath the tan, his voice strangely unsteady. "You really believe that?"

"Is there any reason I shouldn't? Maybe you consider your behavior on-the-job training, but I'm not interested in that kind of education and I never will be! I've told you before—to me you're just one big turnoff, and if you can't get that straight, you can keep your job!" She hoped her Dutch courage would hold until he was out of the room.

"A turnoff?" For a fleeting instant his expression seemed almost vulnerable but it quickly hardened into his typical mocking gaze. He gave a quick shrug, as if to say the whole matter was far too trivial to pursue, and briskly strode to the connecting door. He flung it open, reached around, and plucked a key from the lock. "Here." He tossed it past her to the disheveled bedspread. "You will find a matching key in your dresser. Keep both. Tuck them under your pillow. I wouldn't want you to spend the rest of the day quaking in fear for your virtue. Don't worry, it will be as safe as if surrounded by a moat. I happen to like my women with some degree of sophistication."

Then he went around the door, closed it firmly after him. From the other side she heard him

78

say, "Go on, lock up, infant." Then a brief, almost bitter laugh.

With shaking fingers Penny turned the key and heard the obedient click of the lock. She leaned against the paneling, her heart thudding so violently she wondered if he could hear it on the other side of the door—hear it spelling out how devastated the scene had left her, how her lips still burned from his kiss . . .

Jet lag or no, what had happened on that bed—or rather, what *could* have happened— made it impossible for her to calmly curl up and take a nap. She unpacked hurriedly. Then, with shaking fingers, she brushed her hair and renewed the lipstick his kiss had wiped away. A walk might calm her, the beauty of Paris might help sort out her thoughts.

This could well be her only opportunity to see the city. It was obvious she wouldn't be working for Pierce Reynolds for any length of time. There was just too much tension between them. Could she have unwittingly lured him on? Had he sensed the immense physical attraction she felt every time he came near her?

That kiss, that brief, heart-stopping interlude on the bed, could it possibly have meant anything to him? How could it not, when it had shaken her so, given her her first real taste of burning desire? Like being reborn, her body had seemed to emerge from a deep sleep. Wonderful sensations had quivered along her skin, roused every nerve. . . . She had felt for a moment as if she were on fire, and yet she hadn't wanted to move from the mounting flames—for a moment she hadn't wanted to escape. . . .

Was this what all the love songs were about? All the songs she had sung and played without having the slightest idea of what they meant?

Paris knew what they meant, she realized, as she moved out onto the sun-filled, people-filled Champs Elysées.

She had never seen anything like it—the city teemed with lovers. Although it was a working day and only midmorning, lovers stood in the doorways of shops and restaurants, holding hands, smiling at each other; lovers leaned against the chestnut trees and gazed soulfully into each other's eyes; and near a Metro kiosk a couple stood locked in an unrestrained and seemingly eternal embrace. They all seemed to be saying, *In Paris 'l'amour' comes first*.

An incident at the street crossing was the most startling of all. Penny was standing at the curb when a man ran up to a car, leaned in and kissed the dark-haired girl driver just before the light changed! And as he performed his daring deed loud cheers went up from the other motorists! And strangest of all, the girl who was kissed wasn't even indignant! In fact, she sped off in her tiny car with a smile lighting up her piquant face!

I guess I'm not very sophisticated, Penny thought, and then heard the echo of Pierce's words—*I like my women with some vestige of sophistication*.

Why then had he tried to make love to her? He certainly couldn't have been inflamed by her beauty. Despite his compliments, she knew she wasn't like the girl on the Folies Bergère posters, a girl audaciously proud of her seminudity and her vigorously developed body. Alongside that girl she would look as anemic as a lily in a rose garden.

But, of course, Pierce Reynolds was a man who believed in instant gratification. By now he probably had completely put out of his mind the embrace that had so fired her. How she wished she could be that airy, be like the laughing girl motorist, for whom a kiss held as much weight as the fluff of a dandelion!

The thing she had to do, she thought miserably, was remember that there *were* other men in the world, millions of them. Maybe right here on the Champs Elysées there was a lonely but irresistible Frenchman who not only would thrill her with his kisses, but be thrilled in return!

"Bonjour, Mademoiselle, quel beau temps!"

A hand touched her arm and Penny turned, startled, then broke into a smile. He wasn't a Frenchman, but she was glad to see him anyway. "Oh, it *is* a lovely day, Mr. Carpenter! Or should I say Captain?"

"John would be even better—although I'm flattered you remember *any* vital statistics. Unfortunately I can't return the compliment, you never told me your name."

"I'm Penny Marsh."

"*Enchanté*. And in plain English, very glad to see you." John Carpenter's gray eyes were as warm as she remembered them from their brief encounter in the aisle of the 747. "I thought you said you weren't headed for Paris."

"I wasn't originally." She walked comfortably alongside him. He was out of uniform and looked relaxed in cream-colored corduroy slacks and a maroon turtleneck sweater. "My boss changed his plans, I'm going to Vienna tomorrow."

"Well, I'm grateful to your boss. Where are you headed at the moment—mind company?"

"Not if you don't mind seeing the Arc de Triomphe. I had a French grandfather who was a war veteran. I feel I ought to visit the Tomb of the Unknown Soldier."

"You'll need a tomb yourself if you use this route."

"But someone told me it's at the end of this street!"

He motioned to the wildly converging traffic. "Would you believe no less than twelve avenues radiate from this arch? That means *cars*, all driven by people who never heard of speed limits!" He took her arm. "Let me lead you through my dark, secret passage."

Penny laughed. "Via the Casbah, Captain?"

Taking her arm, he escorted her toward a stairway and into an underground passage. It led them directly up to the giant stone archway from which the city fanned out in all directions. They circled the monument, studying the martial scenes and John pointed out the list of

Napoleon's victories. "Much prettier at night when it's illuminated. But, hey, this is sober stuff for your only day in Paris. You should be strolling on the Left Bank, it's what Paris does when the sun comes out."

It was true. The Left Bank was crowded with promenaders of all ages, in all kinds of costumes from worn jeans to gold-threaded saris. Some people munched on waffles, a favorite Parisian sidewalk food, John said, others walked with faces hidden in books. Artists lugged paints and easels, looking for a fresh vantage point from which to work, and tourists waited to board picturesque boats floating on the river.

"Hey—you're being widely appreciated," John said, smiling.

"*Stared* at, you mean! What *is* it? Am I breaking out in spots or something?"

"Don't you know the French male is constitutionally incapable of being blasé about a pretty face? If you were alone, you'd very soon collect yourself an escort—maybe two or three. It's your coloring. They're mad about blondes."

"It's nice to have somebody mad about me." Without meaning to, Penny had let a mournful note creep into her voice.

John peered intently at her. "Carrying a torch?"

She hesitated. All at once she felt a terrible need to talk to someone about it. "I guess you could say that."

"Is it Reynolds? I hope not."

"How . . . how did you know?"

"Saw you on the plane with him. I've had him aboard a few times. He's the fellow who made a fortune buying up condominiums when everybody said they were doomed. A shrewd investor —at least, that's what I read in the financial pages."

"You know more about him than I do."

"Girl in every city, I hear."

"Really?" Penny said over the lump in her throat.

"Well, stewardess chatter. . . . I feel sorry for men who lead such high-pressured lives."

"Isn't flying high-pressured?"

"Not for me. It's given me some exciting adventures—in fact, all I need for the rest of my life."

"That sounds as if you're tired of flying."

"Not really, but suddenly I don't want to be rootless any more. I want a house in one spot, a garden, a family, a pretty wife." He laughed. "Preferably a pretty *blond* wife—see, I'm the same as the French! So that's what I plan to do very shortly, settle down."

"With a gorgeous stewardess?"

"I doubt that. The ones I've met so far aren't interested in a little house and a family. They're out for glamour, money, the rich boys like your boss."

"That isn't fair to stewardesses. I'm sure they have their share of idealism. I'm sure many of them have a strong sense of values."

John tightened his hold on her hand. "That's what people need most, isn't it? A sense of values. And see what a good judge I am? I knew I'd take to your values the minute I saw you."

Behind the light tone of voice and the smiling eyes, Penny realized he was trying to tell her that he could be very interested in her. He was a thoughtful, nice person, she decided. Someone who would give her a straight answer. "John," she said in a low voice, "tell me something: Why would a man treat a woman in a very ambivalent way—blow hot one second and cold the next? What's the reason behind it?"

"Is that how Reynolds treats you?" John studied her face. "Penny, take my advice—stay away from him. Let him break the stewardesses' hearts—they're made of sterner stuff, they've seen more of the world. You're not a bouncing-back type."

"But . . . can't you answer my question?"

"Well, sometimes a man is afraid to show his real feelings, sometimes he's not even sure of them."

"Not this man! He's not afraid and he's never unsure!"

John was obviously younger than Pierce, but at the moment he looked quite mature. "Penny, everybody in the world is—well, if not afraid, at least uncertain, sometimes. A man could be attracted to a girl, but think she's too beautiful for him or too young . . ."

"No, not in this case."

A woman pushing a baby carriage had come abreast of them. Penny saw her stop, bend over the carriage to adjust her baby's blanket.

"John, *look*—the lady's bread!" Penny cried.

She watched while John rushed to rescue the long loaf which had slipped out of the woman's string shopping bag and was rolling merrily away on the down-sloping pavement.

"Merci, merci, Monsieur!" the woman cried gratefully.

Smiling, John bent to admire the sleeping baby, his expression warm, completely genuine. Penny felt a sudden wistfulness. If only she could get interested in someone like John Carpenter. She could picture him in a little house with roses and a picket fence. A nice, reliable, loving man—one who didn't yearn for power, wasn't inscrutable or arrogant—a *knowable* man with no exhausting temperament, no cruel, bruising passion.

It was even somehow suitable that John preferred chocolate to champagne, she thought, as they stopped at a nearby sidewalk café. But of course this was chocolate like no other she had ever tasted—superbly made from ground chocolate, John said—a café specialty. With it they had an omelet miraculously endowed with the texture of a cloud.

Penny struggled to put Pierce out of her mind as John told her about some of the more exotic passengers he ran into on his intercontinental flights. "One woman always buys three extra plane seats—one for each wig box. She won't trust those wigs to the baggage car. We figure each hair must be twenty-four karat gold."

Penny laughed, buttered another croissant and for a little while her conflicts faded. She felt more carefree than she had in a long time. When she glanced at her watch, she was startled to see they had been sitting at the café table for two and a half hours.

"I love the fact that they let you sit and sit!" she cried. "At home they'd be charging you *rent!* In fact, I love Paris in general, although I still haven't gotten a look at a Paris gown. Not that I could buy one. I just want to moon over one!"

"You don't need that kind of fancy ornamentation."

"That's what *you* think! There isn't a woman in the world who doesn't think of clothes when she thinks of Paris."

"Okay, Mademoiselle—window shopping coming up."

They taxied to the exclusive Rue St. Honoré, stared in at windows displaying tuxedos for boys under ten, and flowers so realistic you couldn't believe they were made of silk.

"I'd buy you a bunch, except that fake flowers are just too cynical for you," John said, and Penny was keenly aware of the admiring warmth of his eyes.

They walked past glittering shops with gowns by Dior, Lanvin and Pucci. But oddly enough it was in a tiny shop on a side street, a shop carrying ready-to-wear, that Penny saw the gown most suited for her. It was a very simply made violet silk, its only decoration a spray of rhinestone stars strung across the front panel of the full skirt. "Just like the Milky Way!" she sighed. "And it looks like my size!"

"Want to try it on? The price isn't bad, for Paris."

"I'm afraid I have to be horribly sensible. I'm not sure how long my job will last. But I'll make a mental note of the name of this place, Madame Lily's. Maybe someday . . ." She looked at John. "Do you think it would make me look sophisticated? A *little*? Maybe?"

He frowned. "Why on earth would you *want* to?" And then his lips folded. "I guess I know why."

When they reached the marble steps leading to her hotel, John said, "Wait a minute!" and hurried down to the flower stall on the corner. When he came back, his lean face was half obscured by a magnificent mass of white lilacs.

"Told you you deserve real flowers." His smile was boyishly self-conscious as he thrust the bouquet at her.

"Oh! Oh, they're so beautiful!" Penny sniffed the dizzying perfume. "You're very sweet."

"Sweet enough to rate your company again tonight? I'll get tickets for the Comédie Française."

"Oh, I'm afraid not, John. My boss wants me on hand to meet some woman who works for him."

"Well, can I see you off for Vienna in the morning?"

"I don't even know what time I'm leaving. He hasn't told me yet."

"I'll phone you later, okay?" He gave the boyish smile. "It was a super day. I hope we can have more of them back in the States."

"I hope so, too." Over the white froth of flowers Penny smiled at him. Maybe it was Paris, but she found herself doing something completely out of character. Standing on tiptoe and in full view of the hotel lobby and passersby, she kissed John Carpenter right on the mouth. And as she did it, she very deliberately let her senses take over, forced her lips to relax, so she could test every ounce of her feelings.

"You're going to have a hard time shaking me after that!" John cried. Obviously elated, he ran down the marble steps as if he were about to break into a polka.

Penny stared at him, and felt her own smile fading. She couldn't fool herself—with John's lips against hers she had felt nothing but the pleasant warmth of human contact. Nothing had lurched in her—her heart had been as still as if it were napping. Her heart that just that morning had learned to sing and soar ecstatically during another man's kiss.

Wearily she pushed at the revolving doors, felt herself being spilled into the lobby—and was startled by a harsh voice in her ear: "So glad you found yourself some entertainment, Miss Marsh. I was afraid you'd be at loose ends, an innocent adrift in wicked Gay Paree!"

Chapter Six

For one foolish second she actually felt guilty.
Standing in the formal marble-walled lobby,
clutching her immense bouquet, she stared up
at Pierce Reynolds as if he were her father and
she a troublesome adolescent coming home past
curfew.

At the same time she was sharply conscious of
her rumpled clothes and windblown hair. It was
late afternoon, a time of formal dress for the
guests at the hotel and Pierce looked elegant and
impressive in his dinner clothes.

"Oh . . . oh . . . ." She made an awkward swipe
at a strand of flyaway hair that dangled on her
forehead.

And then all at once the anger shot up in her.
No one had the right to tell her what to do with
her private hours! Pierce Reynolds hadn't re-
quired her services. She hadn't cheated him in
any way! What right had he to stand there with
that murderous glare on his face?

"Yes, I had a *very* entertaining day, Mr. Reynolds!" Defiantly she waved her bouquet. "Aren't these gorgeous? My friend just gave them to me!"

His eyes were flat as stones. "I see your much-touted determination to operate on a businesslike level doesn't carry over to airline personnel."

"Why should it?" She tilted her head and made her smile taunting. "I don't work for the airlines."

"Behaving the way you just did on the front steps of one of the best hotels in Paris doesn't exactly enhance your professional image."

"Mr. Reynolds, I've just seen duplicates of my behavior right on the steps of Notre Dame Cathedral! In fact, Paris looks like one big Spin-the-Bottle game!" She swung her keys angrily. "And now, if you'll excuse me, I'll get tidied up. You *did* say we're having dinner with your friend, Anne Martel?" She started away, then turned back to him. "Although I hope dinner will find you operating on a more . . ." she fished for the telling word, "a more *sophisticated* level!"

His face went through a whole series of expressions, none of which she had time to interpret, she was still teeming with her own heated feelings. "Mr. Reynolds, sometimes I think the way you act has some *personal* reason behind it!"

"Really?" His lips twitched. "And what would that be?"

91

"Maybe you're annoyed because I'm someone who can't be pushed around." She watched his face closely. "Maybe . . . maybe there's something about my *youth* that bothers you!"

"Your youth." He sampled the thought. "Yes, your youth *would* make quite a chasm between us, wouldn't it?"

Penny suddenly felt deflated. For some reason the words she had said, half to hurt him and half to test his reaction, were now hurting *her*. *The only chasm between us is the space filled by these lilacs! she yearned to cry.*

But he was looking past her at the big gold-filigreed clock.

"You're quite right," he said almost absently, "I do apologize. My only excuse is that this has been a day of immense frustration."

Frustration? Penny flushed, seeing him as he had looked that morning on the bed—the pulse in his throat so visibly excited—he'd been a male repulsed, failing to possess his quarry. She remembered the capsized look on his face.

"I've been frustrated trying to catch up with Anne," he said. "I've phoned all over. And here she's late for dinner. She's never kept me waiting before."

How silly to have thought it was *she* who had frustrated him! Pierce Reynolds, who had long, long lines of women who didn't dare keep him waiting. The thought immediately rekindled Penny's anger. "Yes, I guess that *would* be a new experience in your life! I guess your girl at the

Folies would keep the *curtain* waiting rather than Mr. Reynolds!"

The minute she said it, Penny knew how revealing the words were, knew that from under them peeped the brilliant green hem of her jealousy.

Oh, she was so mixed up! Standing so close to him, seeing the clean cut of his profile, the striking masculinity of his figure in the perfectly cut dinner jacket, she felt a longing that almost choked her. What she wanted more than anything else in the world was to get inside this man, bore a little hole into his mind and see what he was thinking, and a bigger hole in his heart to see what he was feeling!

"I fail to see even the vaguest connection between my *Folies* friend and Anne Martel," Pierce said dryly. "But, of course, you don't know Anne. She happens to be an exceptionally mature and wonderful woman."

"Oh, I'm sure! And I suppose she looks like a dray horse and wears brogans and felt hats, and the two of you sit for hours reading the *Wall Street Journal* together. I can just see it!" Cheeks flaming because now she knew she was losing all control, Penny started to sweep away from him.

And then she was stopped by the smile on Pierce's face, a puzzling bright banner of a smile. Was he going to laugh it all off, rescue her from her own silly blunders?

But then she realized the smile was leaping

past her, traveling across the lobby to the revolving doors, to one of the most striking women Penny had ever seen.

"*Pierce!* Oh, *chérie,* I am *so* happy to see you!"

"Not any happier than I am to see *you*." His voice was warm, his eyes warmer, as he moved to meet the woman and took her arm with easy familiarity. "I was beginning to be very worried about you, Anne."

"I will tell you, darling . . . let me catch my breath!" Her slightly accented voice was husky.

Penny, watching them, wished she could curl up in a corner like a dust ball, or better still, become invisible, so no one could contrast her appearance with Anne Martel's.

Anne wore her thick dark hair in a rich chignon. On some women the style would have looked school-teacherish; on Anne it was a striking foil for her firm classical features and exotic, olive complexion. Her large bronze-colored eyes were almond-shaped, the eyelashes dusky.

She had the French flair for clothes. Everything Anne Martel wore went perfectly with everything else, and all joined hands to stress her femininity. Her dress was a soft rose, cleverly cut to emphasize a good waist and minimize rather full thighs. Her purse and shoes were of the palest beige lizard, and her gold and amber jewelry echoed the unusual color of her Cleopatralike eyes.

Unhappily shifting her lilacs from arm to arm, Penny heard Pierce introducing her and in the mirror saw herself alongside the woman Pierce had called "wonderful."

I look as if I just came from a Girl Scout cookout—smudged chocolate on my lips, grass stains on my skirt, and not a jewel anywhere except my class ring. Oh, I'm a dream boat, all right!

"It's nice to meet you," she murmured hastily in Anne's direction. "And now if you'll excuse me, I must change."

"No time for that," Pierce said. "Our table has been waiting for over an hour."

"Oh, I am so sorry!" Anne spoke with just the slightest accent as, smiling, she hooked her arm in Pierce's. "I have kept you all waiting, it is unforgivable!"

"Unforgivable from anyone but you." Pierce's face was soft.

"Really," Penny struggled, "I look a mess!"

Pierce shook his head without looking at her. "No, you're fine. I want you two to get to know each other and the best place for that is over the dinner table. Besides, I haven't had lunch, I'm famished."

"Oui, j'ai faim aussi!" Anne clung cosily closer to him, giving her shoulders a little shudder, as if she were chilly.

But, of course, she wasn't chilly. The lobby still held the sunny day's warmth. That little shudder, Penny knew, was just a way of wiggling closer to Pierce.

Miserably, eyes on the floor, she walked slightly behind them into the hotel's famous dining room. *He's doing this deliberately*, she thought tightly, *making me come in here looking like this. It's his way of getting back at me*.

But getting back for what? The kiss she'd given John?

Why would he care whom she kissed—unless he cared something about *her*?

Which obviously wasn't the case—not the way he was looking at the elegant woman beside him. The light in his eyes was unmistakably admiring.

As she sat down at the table with them, she was terribly conscious of how comfortable they were with each other. *Odd woman out*, she thought, listening to their half-English, half-French dialogue. As the waiter thoughtfully provided a vase for John's lilacs, Penny stole a quick look around the dining room. It was magnificent, hung with fine paintings, filled with bejeweled, stunning women. . . .

Head self-consciously lowered, she stared at the menu, as Pierce's words cut through her thoughts. "Anne, what in the devil's up? I've been trying to reach you all day! What's happening with our painting?"

Anne's eyelids lowered, an odd expression crossed her striking face. "*Chérie*, I have been working very, very hard on this! I will know the answers tomorrow night. I will be able to give you definite information about the Manet tomorrow night! I will need this one more day to track it down. You know, Pierce . . ." Anne put her jeweled hand gently over his, "I am not at all certain this is truly a Manet. I warn you—do not be too hopeful!"

"Well, of course I'm hopeful." Pierce looked puzzled. "On the phone you seemed pretty sure it was the real thing."

"I was never really sure! But we will see tomorrow. I will go . . . study it again."

"Why can't I go see it, too? Why do I have to wait for your verdict? What's the big mystery?"

"*Chérie please,* it is most delicate! This I must handle. So you take this day or two to enjoy yourself. I have missed you. Why do you take so long to come to Paris and me? I write and write and you do not come!"

Penny looked enviously at the woman. If Pierce wanted sophistication, there it was— Anne Martel, unafraid to express her feelings, to demand attention. Such immense charm, even in a business situation. . . .

Then she was aware of Anne's eyes darting to her, eyes quite cool and weighing—and promptly dismissing. It was obvious Anne didn't consider her any kind of rival—a young girl lacking in chic . . . not even a decent *maquillage*.

"When we have given our order," Anne said, "may I whisk your pretty little helper to the powder room? She would like to arrange her hair, no?"

"That is *exactly* what she would like to do!" Penny said, glaring in Pierce's direction, and when his lips curved in an amused smile, she wished she had the courage to swing her foot out for a painful rendezvous with his ankle. He

97

knew she was feeling miserable, messy and unattractive.

The powder room was black and silver, nostalgic for the Twenties. Anne sat at the dressing table and promptly began to add another coat of mascara to already heavily darkened lashes. As she worked, she talked rapidly to Penny, sketching out her life in a remarkably candid way. She was a widow, had lost her husband some five years ago and Pierce Reynolds had saved her life.

"Yes," she said, "I was so unhappy I wanted to die! You see, we French women of my class are brought up just to be wives—we are absorbed in our men. So when we are early widowed, there is nothing!" She spread beautifully manicured hands. "I knew nothing except cultural things. I had no trade. I am from a wealthy family, I have no need of money," she sighed, "but I need something to *do,* you see? Pierce rescued me, he put me to work looking for things for him, beautiful things. He keeps me busy, fills the days, the many hours of the days."

"I understand," Penny said, wondering what it was all leading to.

Anne Martel turned from the mirror. "He is very important to me, Pierce Reynolds. But sometimes I do not think he knows that. He thinks I am still belonging to Jacques, my husband. I must have some way to tell him I am ready to be a wife again, no sad widow. And tomorrow, his *Bon Anniversaire.*"

"Oh, his birthday?"

"His thirty-fourth. Yes. And that is where I need you, my little one. I need a big favor. I need you to help me keep him occupied tomorrow afternoon."

"I'm afraid I won't be here. I'm leaving for Vienna."

"Oui, you are the violin girl." Anne's full lips made a bunchy smile. "But it is very simple, no? You have a big cold," she picked up a tissue from the mirrored box and held it to her nose, squinting to make her eyes weepy-looking. "Oh, you are so sneezy and headachey, you cannot possibly travel to Vienna, yes?"

"But I don't understand. . . ."

Anne clasped her hands prayerfully. "I beg you! For a lonely widow. . . . You see I must make the plot for this man! The only way I could get him to Paris was this business of the Manet."

Penny stared at her. "You mean . . . there *is* no Manet?"

"No Manet." Anne smiled imperturbedly. "For love we must pretend sometimes, no? For love—you Americans say it—*anything* goes!" She studied her polished face in the mirror. "So now he is here, my darling Pierce, and tomorrow night the Pompadour Ballroom upstairs will be all for him. A party, marvelous, extravagant . . . This is what delayed me today—just yesterday he finally says yes, he is coming. I had only these few hours to prepare, to order the special chef, to be fitted at the couturier. All day I am so busy, I am getting in touch with all his friends. It will be as splendid as Maxim's tomorrow night!"

99

"Well, that's very nice . . ."

"So Pierce will know he is loved, you see? Is very important. He is a hardworking man, he must take time for love or he will get sick." She twisted the diamond wedding band on her left hand. "As for me, no longer can I live without a husband."

Penny's throat hurt, but she managed to scrape out the words: "Is he . . . is Mr. Reynolds in love with you?"

"Oh!" Anne looked at her with surprised eyes. "But, *mon enfant,* that is of no moment, that can be handled! There is no woman in the world worth being called a woman if she cannot make a man love her. Certainly you know that! Oh, but I forget . . . you are so young, just newly a college girl!"

"Just newly *out* of college," Penny corrected dully. "Aren't you afraid Mr. Reynolds will be . . . upset. I mean, about the painting?"

"Oh, he will be a big angry bear!" Anne made a savage face, then laughed lightly. "But there are ways to make him smile again. Although I should not have said a Manet—he adores Manet! I should have said perhaps a . . . Braque. Then he would not be so eager! so impatient! That is why you must distract him. You will have the sneezies, and he will be too occupied to do what he did today, telephone my office, all over Paris . . . it would end up with him finding out, and that must not happen." She stood up. "I will tell him he must take care of you, as you are so very young and far from home. And then, in the evening, you will feel much better—it will be a miracle!—so you will be able to come to the party. . . ." Her voice turned slightly conde-scending. "You will arrange your coiffure a little, dance a little, be a happy child . . . *parfait.*"

Penny lowered her eyelids. It was plain that Anne had completely discounted her as anyone who could possibly interest Pierce. Otherwise the woman would never be suggesting the kind of arrangement she had described. It was so ironic, Anne enlisting *her* aid to capture Pierce.

But then, of course, Pierce obviously wouldn't mind being captured by such a strong-minded, striking enchantress.

"Miss Martel, really, I don't think I can do this."

But the Frenchwoman was gliding out the door and didn't seem to hear—didn't want to.

Reluctantly Penny followed. She reached the table in time to hear Anne say, "Your little assistant seems to be coming down with *la grippe.*"

"Oh?" Pierce had the grace to pretend con-cern. "I'm sorry, Penny. Can I get you a sweat-er? Shall I order you some hot tea?"

"No . . . no . . ." She looked away, tears well-ing helplessly in her eyes. Suddenly, seeing them together this way, she realized how perfect Anne was for him. She was like another wise investment, a good business asset—a graceful, knowing woman who could be shown off proudly anywhere in the world.

They've probably been having an affair, she

thought, from the way she touches him every minute.

Or did French women normally act that way with a male acquaintance?

"I'll be fine!" she heard herself choke at Pierce. "You don't have to worry—I'll make the plane tomorrow!"

"That's the farthest thing from my mind." Pierce stood up. "I'm going to call the hotel physician."

"No! I just need some aspirin—some rest! If you'll just excuse me . . ." She reached blurredly out for her flowers.

"Yes, you certainly mustn't forget your admirer's offering." Was there a sarcastic edge to his voice? It didn't matter, Penny thought, nothing mattered now. She just wanted to get away from the sight of the two of them, looking so right together.

"I'll see you to your room." Pierce's fingers closed on her elbow.

"No, please! Go on with your meal, I'll be fine."

Bundling the lilacs to her chest, she swerved away, evading his eyes, and caught Anne's amused expression—*The child is carrying this act a little too far, giving up her dinner.*

Let Anne think whatever she wanted.

Let both of them think what they wanted.

Penny knew what she had to do.

She wasn't going to be used by Anne Martel in her little game. She wasn't going to stay around and see Pierce's birthday celebration flower into a giant engagement party.

Penny Marsh was going home. It was all too much to handle. And although she realized leaving without doing what she had been hired to do wasn't fair—after all, it wasn't Pierce's fault that she was so idiotically in love with him—still, she had no choice. She would return the money he'd given her for expenses, and as soon as she had another job, she'd pay back her plane fare and anything else he had spent on her.

She hurried to her room. She might have to use her connection with John Carpenter to get a last-minute reservation, but she knew she could count on his help.

Sinking down on the satin-sheathed bed, she stared up at the ceiling mirror—remembering the passion of the morning, the brief moment when she was a nymph and he a satyr and she had felt as if they were teetering on the brink of something glorious, unforgettable. . . .

Miserably she looked away, moved to gaze down at the courtyard, alive now with lighted lanterns, couples sitting close, sipping wine.

Oh, Paris, how I hate to leave you! You're the city of lovers—and you'll always mean Pierce to me!

And I'll never see either of you again.

The thought ripped her apart. Not to see Pierce again! Never to look into those unknowable dark eyes that seemed to want to probe every part of her.

Not to see him again would be like taking the sunlight out of her world. It would be living with an ache that never diminished, a heart too benumbed ever to leap or dance or thrill again.

The telephone rang at the precise moment she reached for it. John Carpenter. Could he escort her to her plane tomorrow? Or, even better, could he use his last day of vacation to go along with her to Vienna, just for the ride?

She fully intended to tell him she was going in the opposite direction and heading home.

Fully intended to, but couldn't. Her lips wouldn't frame the words.

How could she give up the gift Anne Martel had so unwittingly offered—the chance to be alone with Pierce for a few final hours.

A chance to look at him, be close to him, with everything else shut out. How could she give that up?

It will be my souvenir, she thought, *like the lock of hair old-time heroines cherished to keep their lost loves alive.*

That memory would be all she would ever have of Pierce.

"John," her voice trembled, "I—I'm not going tomorrow. I . . . I've come down with a cold, a terrible cold."

Then she closed her eyes, listening to John's concern. Couldn't he come over tomorrow, keep her company, bring her things? If she hadn't been buffeted with so many complicated feelings, Penny would have laughed at the crazy humor of it—*two* men coddling her for a cold that didn't exist! But, of course, Pierce would be with her not out of choice, but only because Anne had asked him to.

She told a disappointed John that she planned to spend the next day in bed, and again promised to see him in the States.

The moment she hung up, the phone rang again. This time Anne's velvety voice purred at her. "So early in the evening, but already Pierce is tired. It is obvious the poor man needs a wife! Now, *ma petite,* I have made him promise to come be your *docteur* tomorrow. He was very agreeable, *très gallant.* He will knock on your door at noon." She laughed. "It is good, being a woman, no? The men, they are so *funny* . . . so *docile* . . . so *amenable.*"

Docile? Amenable? *Pierce?*

Yes, when a clever woman like Anne was doing the maneuvering.

Penny felt a tear move like an uninvited guest along the curve of her cheek.

And then suddenly she was sitting bolt upright.

There is no woman in the world worth being called a woman if she cannot make a man love her.

Famous last words of Anne Martel?

Had the Frenchwoman, without knowing it, been educating Penny Marsh? Insignificant Penny Marsh, whom Anne would never in this world picture as a rival.

Penny felt the quick sweet bloom of hope. Why not? Why *shouldn't* she try? Try being a woman, try being what Anne was—stalking, wily, devious, sophisticated yet primitive! Alluring—but not just appealing to Pierce's physical nature. She wanted to capture his imagination too, so that he would look at her with the open admiration he turned on Anne.

With a leap of excitement, she dialed John Carpenter's hotel. Would he do her a small favor? "Anything," John said. And as she went on to explain, Penny faced up to the ironic fact that if, by some twist of fate, she won at the game she intended to play, she'd still be a loser. Because Pierce Reynolds would eventually break her heart. She knew that.

And she didn't care.

She was as hopelessly enslaved as Linda had been. Had Linda come to the same conclusion—that a broken heart was better than an inert, leaden one and infinitely better than a heart that had never been touched at all?

Chapter Seven

It had been a hectic morning, but when she heard the knock on her door Penny made her voice carefully languid, a complete contrast to her accelerated heartbeat.

"Come id." She was carefully sniffly, too.

"This a convenient time to call?" He stood awkwardly on the threshold, a typical male, uneasy about sickness, vaguely resentful of it.

"I'm happy for the company!" She reached for a scented pink tissue, one of the props in her little drama.

And it *was* a drama, complete with a glamorous setting, beautiful costume, and a leading lady playing the role of a suffering invalid.

Plus a hero who had no idea he was even on stage!

Her lips curled in a small smile, but it faded quickly as she came face-to-face with her own audacity.

She had spent a sleepless night, plotting this moment. After all, if Anne Martel could weave devious designs, why couldn't Penny Marsh?

When morning finally came, she had sent the bellboy out for the scented tissues, the medicines and a fat bottle of *Suivez-Moi*.

After that, she had washed her hair and set it in soft, loose waves around her face. She'd creamed every part of her body, manicured her toes and fingers. She'd sprinkled perfume on every light bulb in the room, then turned on all the lamps to spread the fragrance everywhere.

Next she'd put on the fragile ivory nightgown that had been an extravagant whim back in her college days. She'd never before taken it out of its tissue paper nest. As the gown slithered over her, she was startled to see how it emphasized her gold and turquoise coloring and her fragile, yet rounded, figure.

Over it she draped her creamy velvet robe. Gold evening sandals, she decided, would be more seductive than ordinary bedroom slippers.

Finally she'd devoted a full hour to her face—creaming and moisturizing it, applying a deeper, more dramatic makeup than usual, and just a touch of rose on the tip of her nose for her cold's sake.

Looking in the mirror she had seen a shimmering girl who surprised her.

No, not a girl, a *woman*.

A woman who, for the first time in her life, had dressed with just a special man in mind. Surprising how much difference that made, the exultant, expectant look it lent her eyes.

And now she was ready for the curtain to go up. She lay stretched out on the gold chaise by the window, aspirin and cough medicine prominent props at her elbow, and hoped she could carry her plan through to its final stages, and the very final stage depended on John Carpenter. Maybe it wasn't fair, asking John to give up part of his last vacation day in Paris to run errands for her, but as Anne Martel had said, "When it comes to love, anything goes!"

Anne. . . . At the moment Anne was acting out her own little contrived drama. Supposedly tracking down the Manet, she was actually five floors above them, hard at work in the Pompadour Ballroom, supervising table decorations and handling a temperamental chef. Anne was taking a terrible chance. Suppose Pierce bumped into her in a corridor; then Anne would be the one getting the surprise!

But, of course, clever Anne would bring off such a calamity with a flourish, Penny thought enviously.

Now, looking across the room at her unknowing victim, Penny found that thinking of Anne Martel somehow stiffened her own determination.

Pierce had edged further into the room. "Knocked on your door with a pot of hot tea last night," he said. "I think you were in the shower. But anyway, this is better for you, has more Vitamin C." He held out an elaborate, cellophane-wrapped basket filled with mounds of deluxe oranges and grapes flanking a pretty ceramic pot of honey.

"Oh, how lovely!" Penny remembered to

widen her eyes caressingly. And then she let her hands fall weakly from his offering. "Pierce . . . would you mind putting it over on the table. I feel so . . . so *faint* . . . my *arms* . . ."

"Your *arms*?" He shot her a worried look. "You're not having any *pain,* are you?"

"Oh, just a little stiffness . . ."

"I'll get the doctor right now!" He was striding across the room to the phone, his forehead taut.

"Oh, no, please!" Penny sat up quickly. "I don't need a doctor!"

"Don't be silly, you could be coming down with a serious illness."

"No! It's nothing. I *always* get stiff arms when I have a cold!"

"I never heard of a cold symptom like that."

"I know—it's my peculiarity! Please, Pierce—I have this thing about doctors!" She shuddered, she hoped convincingly. "Anyway, I don't even have a temperature, see for yourself!"

Frowning, he moved to the chaise.

As he lay his hand on her forehead, she stared up at him. He was wearing a white V-neck sweater over a tartan plaid shirt and tight white duck trousers. "You look so handsome and holidayish this afternoon," she murmured softly; "hope I'b nod keeping you from habbing lots of fun somewhere."

"Don't change the subject." His voice was gruff. "You *are* a little hot."

"It's just the sun!" she cried, truthfully enough. She waved a scented tissue, then delicately held it to her nose. "I thought maybe the sun would help my arms and . . . and my poor neck!"

"Your *neck*?" He almost shouted the words.

"Don't get so excited . . . it's just a little stiffness." She bent her head, letting her hair fall forward, fully aware of the golden splash it made in the sunlight. "I guess I got chilled walking near the Seine."

"Here . . . let me try some massage. Sometimes it does wonders."

Submissively she kept her head lowered, shifting her body a little on the chaise, so there would be room for him.

He sat beside her, and his cool hands moved along her neck, and now there was a wild upheaval in her chest, it was like the surge and slap of an ocean wave. His fingers kneading her skin were bringing every part of her terribly alive, sending messages to every inch of her body. It was a sublime feeling, and at the same time she could feel her nerves quiver and clamor, aching for some nameless something more.

"This do the trick?" The fingers worked steadily, gently, and now her thigh was burning too, his knee had glancingly touched it.

"Oh, *Pierce!*" her voice sighed out. Helplessly, unconsciously, her body moved closer to his, and the velvet robe parted, showing the sheer ivory silk of her gown, revealing the outline of her curved thigh.

"Very becoming." His voice was low, a little roughened.

Peering through the glinting curtain of her

hair, Penny saw his eyes tracing the line of her white, high-arched ankle in its gold sandal.

"You ought to always wear velvet," he went on in a voice so low she barely heard it. "It's the perfect match for your skin . . . the same exquisite texture."

"Thank you," she murmured and then their eyes met and couldn't seem to part. The fingers at her neck slowed . . . moved in a gentle ballet to part the folds of her robe, and then they journeyed on, curling under the lace bodice of her gown to find and touch her breast, and she was aware of her nipple rising, peaking, living a shameless life of its own. In the silent room she heard his quickened breathing and then his fingers slid down to her waist, pulling her closer against his hardness, and now his touch was trailing fire along her thigh, and she felt her eyelids sealing. Helplessly she clung to him, her body losing its bones, its very self.

And then abruptly all the magic vanished, the hypnotizing fingers deserted her. He stood up, his face taut. "I'm sorry," he said hoarsely. "You must think I'm a man incapable of living up to his promises. The only excuse I can offer is that Paris does this to a man—and you *are* a lovely bit of feminine temptation. . . ." His voice altered, took on a strivingly breezy tone. "As a matter of fact, I didn't fully realize your stellar attractions until last night when we were going into that dining room. You were carrying those flowers up against your face," his eyes moved to the white cloud of lilacs on the dressing table, "you looked like Primavera . . . springtime itself. Anne thought you were charming, too."

The injection of Anne's opinion was like a drop of sour milk in a bottle of cream. It completely invalidated the compliment. It also helped Penny to fight off the insistent, almost frightening clamoring of her body, her poor body which couldn't understand why it had been brought to such a peak of desire only to be so cruelly abandoned.

"How can you *be* so hypocritical?" she cried at him. "You know very well what I looked like last night!"

"What you . . . ?"

"I looked horrible and you know it! I was never so embarrassed in my life. You forced me to go into that dining room looking like a . . . like a *hitchhiker!*"

"I don't know what you're talking about, you looked unbelievably fresh and sweet."

"Fresh and sweet—you mean like a vegetable from the corner grocery? Is that what you mean?"

"What I mean is, you're a lovely creature."

"Sweet . . . lovely! They're words used for babies . . . and old ladies . . . and . . . and puppy dogs!" she cried, and at the same time part of her brain was pondering the strangeness of it all. Yesterday, when she had been mussed and tired and wearing hardly any makeup, he had found her attractive. And now, when she was dressed like a siren, now when she wanted him with every part of her, he was turning away, telling her that *Paris* was the reason behind his behavior.

So much for ruses, she thought bleakly. It had been a silly game anyway, pretending to be sick, aping some seductress when she really wasn't that kind of girl at all.

"Past experience warns me not to pursue this conversation." He moved restlessly. "It will only end in the familiar way, with your accusing me of all kinds of immoral advances. The truth is that in Paris the aroma of *l'amour* gets into your system and can't be ignored."

Penny held back the quick retort that was struggling to come out. What was the point of arguing now? She'd just play out the scene and forget it. Eyes lowered, she said testily, "Your friend Anne is very beautiful."

"Yes." His gaze flitted to the window. "Yes, Anne is an extremely beautiful woman."

"And you have so much in common."

"Anne and I? Yes, we've been very close." His sharp profile seemed troubled. "I wouldn't ever want to lose her. In fact, I'm beginning to think I don't pay enough attention to her wise advice. Last night she told me I looked very tensed up, overworked, and I guess I am. My nerves feel jangled."

"That's the price you pay for being a youthful success story."

"Youthful?" He looked narrowly at her.

"You seem so to me."

"Which makes me almost obliged to believe

114

it's true. I know you're not one to flatter, you never learned to be devious."

Penny felt her cheeks sting. What would he say about her honesty if he knew she didn't actually have a cold? Or was he being sarcastic, had he noticed that she'd dropped her nasal accent somewhere along the way?

"I'm wondering—would you say I'm youthful enough to do a complete turnabout in my way of life?" he said. "Start giving more time to personal fulfillment rather than work?"

A turnabout. Penny avoided his eyes, her throat tightening. Yes, marrying Anne, settling down in Paris, leading Anne's kind of life, more social, slower-paced . . . that would be quite a turnabout.

"I'm surprised you ask me, you're always pointing out how naïve and unknowing I am."

He looked startled. "Have I been that rough on you? I thought I'd been fairly considerate."

"Well, you have, about some things. I mean . . . well, as a matter of fact . . . last night I was thinking I ought to return the check you gave me. After all, I haven't done any work, all I've done is inconvenience you!"

"Don't worry, I'll see that you earn your salary." He was silent for a moment, then added: "If I called you unknowing, it was because you looked so young, almost childish. But somehow now . . . you . . . you look different. Not that you look *old*—" He broke off, clearing his throat. "I mean—"

Penny had trouble hiding her smile. For the first time she had actually flustered him. But he was too strong a man to let himself be bothered for long, already he was smoothing his face out, waving a jaunty hand. "You know what complicates life most? You women!"

"Really?" She leaned back and the folds of her robe parted and once again his eyes moved down the curve of her bare calf. "I should think women would simplify things for a man. After all, we see that he has clean shirts, and potatoes in the cupboard, and we supply warmth on a cold night, beauty to look at, and support when it's needed. Men seem to have realized that down through the centuries, because they've never stopped marrying, have they?"

He rumpled his hair—an unexpected gesture that caught at her heart. "Just the same no man really *wants* to be captured. Not if he's sane! He's caught because the poor fool can't think straight. Women say 'love me' with their eyes, then hold you at arm's length if you come anywhere near! You're left incapable of figuring out if you really love them or if your glands simply need exercise!"

"If you were really in love, you'd know the difference." Penny spoke almost to herself, and sadly, for although it was obvious that this man sometimes felt a momentary pull toward her, undoubtedly he had experienced far more rewarding encounters with other women and was annoyed and disbelieving when she didn't immediately succumb the way others had. But casual love would never be enough for her. Love had to have richness and depth. It had to be fire, yes, but it also had to be music and clouds and poetry . . . and it had to be there in all the seasons of the year.

His eyes were fastened on her, troubled eyes, and full of an odd nakedness, an intense yearning. It frightened her—was he that desperately in love with Anne? *I wouldn't ever want to lose Anne.* How could anyone ever compete with that kind of emotion?

"How?" He was staring down at her. "*How* would you know the difference?"

"Well . . ." Penny swallowed, pinioned by his eyes—"well, when you're in love, it . . . it just *clamors* at your lips! You want to *say* it so much—*tell* the person. It's a kind of sweet, aching burden. Keeping it in actually hurts!"

"Oh? And what other characteristics does this sublime passion have?" His voice had sharpened almost angrily.

"Well . . . well . . ." Why was he staring so? "Well, you can't stop thinking of the person. He's there in your thoughts every minute like . . . like a *burr!* Only a kind of wonderful burr and then, if he kisses you . . . that kiss makes you so certain you could *die!*"

"A kiss?" He was walking back to her.

"Yes, a *kiss!*" she whispered, and suddenly she ached for the return of his lips, thirsted for them. He *had* to kiss her, he just *had* to!

But no firm hard lips met hers, no arms made a circle of love around her, and when he spoke again his face had a remote look. It was as if, for some reason, he had thrown up a barrier between them.

"And the man who delivers these revealing kisses, is he currently on the horizon, or is he the traditional boy back home?"

Penny swallowed the huge lump that seemed to be lodged in her throat and murmured, almost to herself, "Oh, he's on the horizon, all right. Even if he *weren't,* even if he were on another planet, he'd be on *my* horizon. I'm a one-man girl, always will be."

"I see." His eyes flicked to the lilacs on the dressing table. "Lucky man, rating that kind of devotion. He ought to bottle his secret and pass it on to the rest of us."

His voice was light, but his eyes had a bleak look. Penny felt tempted to jump up, gather him to her, comfort him, tell him he didn't have to worry, Anne loved him as much as he loved her.

But that would be foolish—it would be reneging on her promise to fight for him, to ruthlessly make one last stab at winning his love! She owed it to herself to keep up the fight to the last round, right to the moment when she entered that ballroom tonight!

"I never would have imagined you had already experienced the grand passion." Pierce's voice was mocking.

"Didn't you tell me a minute ago that I looked mature?"

"Well, in that outfit you do. There's no doubt there's a woman under that velvet."

"There certainly is!" she said challengingly.

"And this man of yours . . . does he realize the depth of your passion?"

Penny opened her mouth, then foundered, suddenly bleakly aware of reality.

"No," she muttered, almost inaudibly.

"What a blind idiot he must be!" He reached out, touched her hair, for a moment let a strand curl around his fingers. "I would have tasted your sweet offerings long ago if you looked at me the way you look when you think of him. It's the handsome young airline captain, I suppose?" Abruptly he waved a hand, and a nerve danced in his cheek. "Delete that, I have no right to pry. I don't usually, either. Anne's right, I need a vacation. She was suggesting a long cruise to the Greek Isles. Sounds very appealing at the moment."

Again she felt that he was erecting a barrier and speaking from behind it. In a casual voice he began to talk about Vienna, describing the candlelit baroque concerts at the Palais Pallavicini. "They actually wear eighteenth-century costumes and powdered wigs. But that's later, around early June," he said; "you'll have to put it on your list of future things to do."

He said he had made a reservation for her for the following day, "provided you have fully recovered," at one of Vienna's lushest hotels. "Don't fail to ask to see their tablecloth with the embroidered signatures—seven decades of kings and queens and princes." And if she was planning on furnishing a home of her own with her "grand passion," she should make a point of visiting the petit point studios not far from the hotel, "exquisite chair coverings and the like. When I settle down in my permanent home, I'll order from them."

As he talked on, describing other Vienna joys, Penny lay back on the chaise, watching him, and yet trying not to show that she was filling her eyes and mind and heart with him. She had failed in her design to make him love her, his detached manner proved that. And yet . . . hadn't there been something in the air, an intangible something that was more than just physical passion? For a whisper of time hadn't there been something sweet, delicate, full of wonder . . . something faintly like the love she had envisioned? But at the last moment he had firmly resisted. What had clamped a hand on his shoulder, held him back?

Anne, obviously. If only he hadn't met Anne first. If only Anne were a little less perfect.

But now, as Pierce politely telephoned room service for wine and pastries for them, Penny reminded herself that at least she would always have this time to cherish, this wonderful afternoon alone with him, close to him. No one could ever take this joy from her.

As he hung up the phone, she reached out and touched his arm. The fawn-colored hairs along it were soft as moss. "Thank you, Pierce," she whispered.

His eyes were puzzled. "What for?"

"Just . . . just for spending your afternoon

with me, for being so nice today, for being you."

He studied her for a long moment. Then he shook his head. "You're such a puzzlement. A conundrum. A headache." His grin flashed whitely. "A *woman!*"

It was said with a laugh, but suddenly their eyes tangled, and Penny's breath snagged in her throat. His face came closer and he looked almost like a sleepwalker, eyes wide, hazy.

The knock on the door made them both jump as if guilty. Pierce blinked, slowly rose and went to answer it.

"Hi!"

John Carpenter grinned in at them. He had obviously performed the mission Penny had assigned him. He held the shiny pink dress box aloft, like a trophy.

And at the sight of him the moment Penny had been savoring went up in smoke, blasted away by the storming disapproval and utter shock on Pierce Reynolds' face.

Chapter Eight

Her feeling about the gown had been amazingly right, Penny thought, looking with delighted eyes at her reflection in the pier glass. No embroidered or beribboned original would have suited her small frame as much as this simple drift of violet silk. She turned sideways, happy that her waist was so slender, her arms so white and curving.

Then the porcelain-skinned girl in the mirror turned petunia pink remembering the confusing moment of three hours ago: John framed in the doorway with the dress box and Pierce staring disbelievingly at them.

He had obviously concluded that John was buying—*paying for*—her clothes! But what could she have done? Stammer out the truth—that John was only a delivery boy, that she had used a good portion of her expense money to pay for the dress? That she would subtract the amount from her salary?

Anything she could have said would have been terribly embarrassing for all concerned, so she had stood silent, while Pierce glowered at John and then at her, his polluted infant.

No one could possibly call me "infant" to-night, she thought now, looking at the insolently dipping neckline of her gown.

And now the moment had come. It was time to take the elevator to the Pompadour Ballroom.

Suddenly, as she started for the door, Penny was terrified. Would he look at her, really see her? Or would his eyes cling only to Anne? Would Penny Marsh be just a vague someone in the background . . . someone he barely noticed, as Anne and all his friends pressed around, offering toasts? Some sixty people, Anne had said. Friends she and Pierce had in common. Anne had proudly added that even Eric Genet, the popular music hall dancer, would be among the guests.

The elaborately bejeweled and befurred passengers on the elevator were probably some of those guests, Penny thought. She edged herself into a corner, hands nervously kneading her small satin evening purse. Back in her room her appearance had pleased her, but now, surrounded by all these exquisite designer gowns, all these necklaces and bracelets, even tiaras.

"Depuis combien de temps êtes-vous ici, Mademoiselle?"

Penny blinked at the slender sparkling-eyed man with the pointed beard that made him look almost middle-aged until you took in the smooth planes of his face.

"How long have *you* been here, young lady?"

He had changed over to English after taking in her pale Anglo-Saxon complexion. His eyes, which reminded Penny of green olives, traveled boldly from her face to her bare shoulders and down to the curves of her breasts. It was a roguish—no, rapacious look, Penny thought.

"Just two days," she answered quietly, not encouraging him by returning his gaze.

"Ah, then I have missed two whole days of heaven!" The man smote his forehead, portraying enormous grief. Penny was aware that the people in the elevator were murmuring to each other, the women staring curiously and hostilely at her.

Coolly she lifted her chin, trying to convey a sublime indifference.

But her admirer began to hum insinuatingly under his breath, his steady, embracing gaze never leaving her. Embarrassing as it was, it was also like a dose of adrenaline. Penny felt a welcome confidence wash over her as she swept toward the ballroom.

On the threshold she froze, staring at the magnificence.

Anne had pulled out all the stops. The buffet was spectacular, spread out on a table the width of the ballroom. The centerpiece was a high, many-tiered cake with Pierce's name and a big "34" etched in blue icing. Flanking the cake were two striking ice sculptures, one of the American Eagle and the other of the Eiffel Tower. As she edged closer, Penny saw the beautifully decorated offerings that marched down the table in gold-rimmed servers: *boeuf en croûte*, and that next dish had to be duckling in orange sauce, and crêpes oozing their mouth-watering fillings, and the long platter with the highly decorated fish. Maybe that was from the Gironde River, a very special French treat. And weaving between all these delights were little artificial trees, pink shrimp blossoming on every bough.

Behind her there was a low wave of voices, more guests filing in, and now the small orchestra in the corner was tuning its instruments.

All of it added up to a striking testimony to Anne Martel's managerial and social skills. Enviable qualities for the wife of an up-and-coming tycoon.

"Everybody—*écoutez!* Pierce will be coming in precisely five minutes! So you will step back in the shadows, *s'il vous plaît*. It will make the big surprise—"

Anne's voice broke off. She had caught sight of Penny smiling a hello. For a moment the French-woman's face lost its poise, the almond eyes widened in shock.

Shock that turned into an amalgam of resentment, anger and suspicion. "Oh, Miss Marsh," Anne called. Penny noticed that she no longer rated the affectionate *"mon enfant"*—"you will light the candles at the end of the table, *s'il vous plaît*."

"Certainly." Penny pretended not to notice the way Anne's eyes were scraping over her.

Anne edged closer, smiling stiffly. "Your

125

gown, it is stunning—an original?" And then stingingly: "oh, *non*—I see now, the stitches are *machine!*"

Penny had never liked cattiness, and now she had to remind herself that she was in a battle. "Oh," she fired back, in a deceptively airy voice, "stitches—that's one thing a man never notices. He just sees the general effect, don't you think?"

The way Anne's eyes narrowed revealed that she was giving some thought to precisely which man Penny had in mind.

But then there was no more time for talking or thinking.

"He's *coming!*" someone called from the watcher's post at the door.

"Hide!" someone else urged. *"Vite!"*

The guests edged to the sides of the room while Anne floated triumphantly to the door, her billowing gold taffeta whirling at her ankles, her hands outstretched to Pierce.

Then the orchestra swung loudly into "Happy Birthday," and Anne was kissing Pierce, hanging onto his arm, smiling and whispering in his ear, while their friends swooped down, calling *"Bon anniversaire,* Pierce!"

Pierce looked stunned and once, after Anne had whispered something in his ear, Penny saw him pull away and stare down at the French-woman as if in utter disbelief.

She's telling him the truth about the Manet, Penny thought. *I had to get you here some way, Pierce darling. I had to let you know how much*

126

I love you and wanted to be with you on your birthday. . . . Was that what Anne was whispering?

At any rate what she said had apparently satisfied Pierce. After the first shocked reaction, he had relaxed. Now he was smiling, accepting champagne and the toasts from his friends, nodding his approval of the glittering scene, looking around the room.

Penny ducked away from the sight of his smiling face.

How foolish she had been! Just because she was wearing a pretty dress, she had allowed herself to think—to dream—that he would walk away from Anne and like an enchanted prince float into her arms.

"Mademoiselle, may I bring you something to drink?"

It was the man with olive eyes, the man from the elevator.

"No, thank you," Penny said hollowly. The orchestra was finishing a ballad. Out of the corner of her eye, Penny saw Anne floating in Pierce's arms. Blindly she turned to the olive-eyed man. "I *would* like to dance!"

Just as she spoke, the strains of the ballad died and the orchestra began beating out a much wilder number.

"I would love to dance with you, Mademoiselle," her companion said, "but this number, I must dance very fast to this number, it is a . . . how you say . . . a perpetual motion?"

"So?" Penny said.

He shrugged. "If you are sure you can, well, then, we *dance*, Mademoiselle!"

After which puzzling remark, he encircled her waist, and with an expertise immediately apparent, swept her to the dance floor.

And then she wasn't Penny Marsh anymore—she was a bird gliding through stardust, sweeping over the world, dipping and darting and whirling until everything around her was a vast, multicolored blur and all she could feel was the rhythm and control of the man who was leading her, a man so skilled that she was never conscious of taking a step; all the steps flowed into one long lithe rapturous movement that, in turn, became part of the music itself.

"You are the delightful surprise, *chérie*—you dance superbly!" the olive-eyed man said.

"Thank you," Penny panted. "You're pretty good yourself!" The music was ending, but her smiling partner showed no sign of loosening his hold around her waist.

"Don't work the young lady so hard, Eric, she's more or less of an invalid, and she needs her energy. She's got a tough job of work to do for me tomorrow."

Penny felt her heart rear as Pierce came up behind them.

"Oh?" said the olive-eyed man. "I did not know of any connection between you." He made a regretful mouth. "I suppose you have come to claim her, and since it is your birthday, I will have to part with her. But please first make the introduction, *elle est très charmante.*"

"Penny meet Eric," Pierce said in a rather brusque voice. "And never let him give you a ride in his Maserati, not if you want to live to see *your* next birthday."

Eric bowed, smiling intently at Penny. "Mademoiselle, I relinquish you for the moment, but I am claiming you again very shortly. You are . . . what we French call . . . *ineffaçable.*"

"I don't know that word," Penny said.

"It means . . . it means . . . your name is written here," Eric placed his hand over his heart, "in the indelible ink."

"What a nice compliment!"

Eric raised her hand to his lips. "I will see that you receive others of similar quality."

"All right, you've said your piece." Pierce's voice was light, but his hand circled Penny's waist and tightened. She could see he was trying to edge her away. Very deliberately she rooted her feet to the floor. "I really enjoyed dancing with you, Eric."

"Be surprising if you didn't," Pierce said gruffly. "He's only the highest paid dancer in France."

"You mean . . . ?" Penny clamped a hand over her mouth. *"Eric! You're not Eric Genet?"*

"You mean you didn't *know?*" Pierce laughed, and Eric joined in.

"Yes, I am Eric Genet, and this is Eric Genet's favorite disco number." The dancer reached for Penny.

129

"Hold on, Eric; this is my inning," Pierce said.

"This number is not for you, Pierce," Eric said, "is too fast, too wild for thirty-four-year-old legs."

Penny caught the tightening around Pierce's eyes. "That's silly, Mr. Genet; Pierce can dance to this just as well as anyone!"

Pierce stepped away from her. "No, Eric's right, this number isn't my style."

"Now, just a minute!" Penny's voice was so loud the other dancers turned to stare. "You both act as if I'm some kind of . . . *package* to be passed back and forth! I'll have you know I pick my own partners!" Commandingly she raised her arm to curve along Pierce's shoulder.

Eric spread his hands resignedly. *"Bon anniversaire*, Pierce. And you, Penny, I will catch up with you, you will see. Perhaps you will go for a midnight spin in my Maserati?"

"That's one thing she *won't* do. I don't like to see my employees on crutches!" Pierce smiled, but not with his eyes.

After that Penny scarcely noticed anything. She was snuggling in the circle of Pierce's arms, smelling the wonderful scent of him, masculine and compelling. "Happy birthday, Pierce," she said dreamily. "Thank you," he said. He smiled down at her, and although he lacked Eric's professional skill on the dance floor, they moved together, clung together, as if joined in some ancient love ritual. She felt the taut hardness of him pressing against her, and it seemed as if the arms holding her were so powerful that nothing in the universe could ever come near enough to hurt her. She closed her eyes, helplessly yearning to burrow even closer.

"You certainly made Eric Genet's eyeballs spin," Pierce said lightly. "You know, in Paris he's regarded as irresistible by the ladies."

"Not by this lady."

"Really? Oh, that's right, I forgot your theme song: 'I'm Just a One-Man Girl.'" His lips quirked mockingly. "Well, you've got yourself a nice young fellow. He's a lot safer than Eric."

"*Who's* a lot safer?"

"Your man, Carpenter. We had a drink together in the bar this afternoon. He's pretty crazy about you. Oh, and by the way I apologize, I was awfully stuffy about that business with the dress."

"I thought maybe . . ." she made her voice light, but she was watching his face, "maybe it was old-fashioned male jealousy."

Again she saw the nerve leap in his cheek, the eyes turn flat. "That would be a pointless reaction, wouldn't it? I guess the idea of somebody buying you clothes didn't jibe with my conception of you. But John told me you asked him to be your delivery boy because you were too sick—" He broke off, looking down at her. "You've recovered very quickly."

"Oh! I—I took lots of medicine! I'd promised Anne to help out here if she needed me."

"I suppose you knew about the Manet that

131

wasn't?" He shook his head. "I never guessed. In fact, the way Anne was acting had begun to worry me."

"But you're happy now, aren't you?"

"Of course, who wouldn't be? Although I guess I was a little hard on Anne at first—you know, disappointed about the Manet. I lost my sense of what should have top priority."

She stared at his shirt front. "I'm sure Anne knows she has top priority with you."

"I hope so. Giving things their rightful priority is one of the most important things we do." His face was sober. "I hope you're careful, Penny. I hope you don't let life rush by you, don't put off having the fullest life possible. Anne has made me realize my age, and how a person's choices are narrowed down with the passage of every year. Actually, I never really felt old until a few minutes ago, watching you and Eric . . . I was envious. But it's funny, I was proud, too."

"Proud?"

"I guess that's the word. Almost a paternal reaction."

"Paternal?"

"Doesn't that word suit you?" He looked searchingly at her, then looked abruptly away. "All right, let's just stick to plain proud. There you were charming the whole room with your grace—I felt as if your triumph were also mine. Admittedly a strange reaction, I'm usually involved only with my own successes."

Penny felt the helpless tremble of her lower

lip. Resting her head against his shirt front, she heard the muffled drumbeat of his heart. "I think . . . I think it's *nice!*" she choked. "I think it means you like me more than you know!"

"Of course I like you." He smiled obliquely. "I'm not an ogre, you know. I like graceful pretty things . . . who doesn't?"

"You make me sound like a little package from a gift shop."

"I'm sure you wouldn't want me to use more extravagant phrases. You know you wouldn't trust them. And maybe you'd be right. There's something about you that turns me into a bounder." He smiled again, but his eyes remained intent, serious. Then abruptly his arms fell away from her; he let his feet lose interest in the music. "I'd like to see you alone after this is over—don't retire early. I'll bring you your plane tickets and review your duties in Vienna. You *are* up to leaving tomorrow, aren't you?"

"Yes, I'm up to it. But . . . it seems a thousand years since we talked about buying the violin."

"It *was* a thousand years. This has been a very eventful trip for me. In fact, I have a feeling it may change my whole life." His eyes flitted over her face. "Penny—"

"*Chérie!* Your birthday dinner is waiting!" Anne swooped close, skirt caught majestically over one arm, diamond earrings glittering. Hooking her free arm in Pierce's, she dipped toward Penny, squinting. "Oh, *pauvre enfant!* Such a terrible black streak all the way down your little cheek! The dancing makes your eye-lashes run, non? Sometime I tell you the mascara we French use—*c'est parfait!*"

Actually, her mascara looked as perfect as it had when she entered the ballroom, Penny discovered, returning to her room a few minutes later. Anne had simply wanted her removed from the scene. Anne's sharp eyes had apparently taken in quite a lot.

Well, she could relax. The Frenchwoman had very obviously snagged her prize, had cleverly convinced Pierce that it was time to settle down, that he was getting too old to go on being a man-about-town. *This has been a very eventful trip for me,* he had said. But why had he added "Penny" in that low, tense voice, what had he intended to say?

Whatever it was, he would probably make clear when he delivered the plane tickets. Penny sank on the chaise, hearing the faint strains of the orchestra floating down from the ballroom. The evening was young, but she felt no desire to go back to the party, to watch Pierce and Anne together.

Don't retire early, her lips flickered wryly, remembering that once before Pierce had given her that kind of peremptory instruction . . . the night he had canceled dinner with her.

And then, as the minutes passed, she found history really repeating itself. The orchestra had stopped playing, elevator doors grated and clanged, discharging guests called out their good nights, the yellow moon was rising over the courtyard, but there was no knock on her door, no sound or light in the adjoining apartment. . . .

Finally, heavy-lidded and moving woodenly, too tired to be angry, she packed for the morning's flight to Vienna. She was undressing when the telephone rang. "Sorry to be calling this late," Pierce said. "I just came back from taking Anne home. After hosting such a splendid evening it would have been ungrateful of me to hurry my good-bye."

"Naturally," Penny scratched, with a quick glance at her clock. His good-bye had apparently taken almost two hours—and Anne's mid-Paris apartment was just a short ride away—she remembered Anne saying it was near the Place Vendôme.

"I have your tickets here, along with some suggestions about getting around Vienna," he went on. "Should I leave them at the front desk for you to collect in the morning or . . ." his voice lowered . . . "or could you possibly see me now? Your light's showing under my door, so I figured you were still awake."

Penny's eyes moved to the connecting door and its yellow margin of light. She swallowed, and her hand tightened on the telephone wire. If he decided not to join her in Vienna, it would be such a long time before she saw him again! Maybe he wouldn't even fly back to the States with her. Maybe he'd decide to stay behind with

135

Anne, and then the immense expanse of the Atlantic would lie between them . . . perhaps forever. . . .

"I . . . I guess I'd better go over everything with you," she heard herself say shakily.

She had just enough time to run to the closet and snatch up her peignoir, a demure pale blue drift of cotton. She sashed it tightly over her wispy beige bikini panties.

His knock sent her pulses into a frightened dance. "Coming!" she called hoarsely. She had pulled her hair back into a ponytail and her face was washed free of its evening glamour—and maybe that was just as well, she told herself wryly.

Not that it mattered. As he entered the room, he barely glanced at her. All his concentration was on the sheaf of papers in his hand. Sitting in one of the chairs near the window, he handed her her plane tickets and a page of notes in his bold, dark handwriting. "Now, look," he said, "some very important matters have come up here, so I'm not at all sure I'll be able to join you in Vienna. I want you to keep in close touch with me. And if Muller hints he wants more than the top figure I gave you, please telephone me immediately."

"Of course. Will you still be here at the hotel?"

"Yes. Yes, most of the time." He ran his hand over his forehead in a strangely weary gesture. "Now have yourself a good trip. Too bad your fellow had to fly back to the States, he was quite cut up about that."

136

"Oh—oh, John. Yes."

There was a brief silence and for the first time he looked directly at her. The smile that formed on his lips was different from those she had seen before . . . it had an odd, bemused, reflective quality. "You *are* a child, after all, aren't you? A child and a siren, wrapped into one. I can't tell which I like best . . . this little scrubbed shiny face or the sensuous lady I danced with just a short while ago. I have the unfortunate feeling that I respond to both."

For Penny the moment was one of pure beauty. She felt a joy leaping in her—this was what she had yearned to hear, words like these, that had their origin in his heart.

"Why do you say unfortunate, Pierce?" she asked waveringly.

He stood up, his movements oddly jerky. "Because I want you—you know I want you! It doesn't make a shred of sense, but there it is—I never expected it!"

"But . . . isn't love always unexpected?" Her voice was made frail by the look of desire on his face.

He gave a groan—"don't ask questions like that! Just let me hold you again! I haven't been able to shake off the memory of you in that mirror!"

In one swift movement, he scooped her up; in a breath's time he covered the four feet to the bed. "Pierce—oh, Pierce!" she gasped, but her voice was barely a whisper, she was drowned by his nearness, the scent of him enveloped her and the strength of him weakened her. He carried her as if she were a flower.

And lowered her as gently, onto the bed. Bending over her, he parted the lapels of her robe, spread them wide, and sat for a moment gazing at her pink-tinged flesh. He smiled up at the ceiling mirror. "This is the most beautiful sight a man could see, and I have it in duplicate."

And then he covered her body with his own, kissing her lips, her throat, her breasts, and there was nothing Penny could do. There was a burning sensation all along her limbs and as his kisses covered her flesh, seeming almost to feed upon it, she felt her hands reach out, automatically twine around him. Her fingernails clutched at his back, wanting to find the flesh under the satiny dinner jacket, and suddenly she knew with a driving certainty that in a moment, in just a moment, she would merge with this man, actually become a part of him, linked to him in the sweet ruthless turbulence of desire.

"So pale, so beautiful . . ." His breath caressed her ear. "I've *got* to have you!"

Suddenly the phrase, the driving insistence of it, made her stiffen. How foolish she was, telling herself he was thinking of her as someone special. *I've got to have you!* Yes, that completely expressed the man. The desire for possession was his primary emotion. He coveted her, the way he coveted famous paintings or beautiful instruments, or the fine cars and clothing he owned.

While I was in Paris, I bid in on a cute little thing . . .

Was that the way he would talk about her if she gave herself to him now?

She twisted under his weight, saw his lean, tanned face looking down at her, the hungry lips still wet from the moisture of her own mouth.

"No!" She jerked away from him on the bed, raised herself on an elbow, struggling to cover her exposed body. "I don't want it—I don't *want* it, Pierce!"

"Oh, yes, you do!" His hand grasped her arm cruelly, trying to force her back down against the coverlet. "You want it—it screams out of you!"

"That's . . . that's just . . . just physical!" Her voice was strangled. "What you can't seem to understand is, I exist outside my body! That's why I can't—I *won't*—" Tears sprang in her eyes, and she gazed pleadingly up at him. There was no way she could really be angry with him, not when just a moment ago she had wanted overwhelmingly to become part of him. "Please see." She dropped the words weakly. "Please understand."

"I understand." He jerked away from her and sat up, on the edge of the bed, his handsome dinner jacket rumpled. "Oh, I understand all right." His lips twisted. "What I understand is, Anne was right—I'm *not* myself. If I were in my right mind, I'd never get all riled up about someone like you. I called you a child a minute ago, but I see now how wrong I was. You're not a child—you're a professional tease."

She stared disbelievingly at him.

He wasn't looking at her—he was just sitting there, shaking his head. "Tonight of all nights— what a fool I am! Just because you put that seductive expression in your eyes—what do you do, practice it every morning in front of your mirror? Does it give you a high, seeing a man bowled over by you? Do you get a thrill when he goes berserk with wanting you? Is that your favorite parlor game?"

Listening to his voice, so harsh it was almost unrecognizable, Penny felt as if the universe were toppling around her. The miraculous glow of passion and love she had felt seemed remote, an ancient memory. With a tremendous effort she got off the bed, sashing her peignoir tightly around her. "I don't think you'd better say any more, Pierce." She dredged up the words from a dry, aching throat.

"Why? The truth hurt? You're aware of what you do to me, looking at me as if you want me to consume you! You enjoy it, don't you, messing up my life?"

"*Messing up your life*? Is that what you think?" She struggled to keep her lips from trembling. "Well, don't worry—it won't happen again! I'll finish this job for you because it's my responsibility, and then you won't ever have to see me again. I'll just find some other poor defenseless male to set on fire! You aren't much fun, anyway. You're really not my style!"

His eyes blazed anger, but his cheeks had paled. She sensed her words had found their mark. He stood up, staring at her over the width of the tumbled bed. "Crazy, isn't it? For a while I talked myself into believing you were innocence itself—fresh and pure and beautiful . . ."

"I do put on quite an act, don't I?" Penny made her smile mocking. Because the hurt was unbearable, every part of her was stinging under the lash of his unexpected accusations.

"You certainly do, lady!"

He spun on his heel. Dazedly she watched him stalk to the door, his jaw set, his eyes steely. Suddenly it seemed intolerable that he should leave carrying with him this distorted, ugly image of her. An image that she, in her hurt and anger, had helped reinforce.

"Pierce—Pierce, please don't go!" The ragged words fell from her lips, but they came too late and were obliterated by the loud slam of the door as he made his exit. She ran to the door, then stopped and leaned against it, her whole body shivering. Should she follow him, make him listen?

But what was there to say? He had already indicated his regret at entangling himself with her, "tonight of all nights," he had said, obviously referring to the purpose of Anne's party. In all probability he was now formally engaged to the Frenchwoman.

A tease. The words echoed and re-echoed in her mind. And she remembered how, just a few minutes ago, her body had spilled out unmistakable messages of love and desire. Maybe she *was* a tease. Maybe his reaction was typical of any man brought to the brink of passion and then denied release. Maybe by responding so wholeheartedly to his kisses she had seemed to be making promises.

One thing was certain—today had marked the end for her and Pierce Reynolds. *You aren't much fun, anyway*—the mocking words would probably echo in his mind whenever he thought of her.

"*Ohhh*," she moaned sickly, biting her lips and pressing her head against the hard panel of the door. Listening to the heavy thud of her heart, she felt like someone shipwrecked. Someone who knew she was destined to spend the rest of her life gazing hopelessly at a beautiful, far-away, forever unattainable shore.

Chapter Nine

The bellboy carried her suitcase into a room done in mulberry and antique white. The canopied bed had marvelous baroque carvings on the posts and an unbelievably puffy mattress. A huge oil painting featured a rather fleshy lady running through the woods, dropping her chiffon undergarments after her. In the distance a handsome prince smiled his approval. Romance had invaded even the bathroom: thick mulberry towels were proffered by a four-foot marble cupid, and the tub was decorated with hand-painted hearts and flowers.

And from somewhere, faintly, Penny caught the muted lilt of a Strauss waltz. Vienna, a city drenched in music, the place so dear to Mozart and Schubert, the place she'd always dreamed of seeing.

And now she didn't care. Someone had dropped a veil over the world, a gray coarse veil, robbing everything of life and color and meaning.

The truth, she knew, was that she was only physically in Vienna. The parts of her that mattered were still in Paris. Standing at the window, looking out at Vienna's lovely Stadtpark, she kept seeing the Champs Elysées, kept imagining Pierce and Anne at a sidewalk café, laughing, touching, planning their honeymoon trip to the Grecian Isles, deciding where they would live when they returned. *A place on the outskirts of Paris, darling?* Anne would say. *Just far enough out to have a decent garden?*

A small sound brought Penny back to reality, the bellboy clearing his throat meaningfully.

"Oh!" She dug in her purse. "Thank you. *Vielen Dank!*" She held out the tip. "*Trinkgeld?*"

The word acted like an electrical charge. The boy, wearing an ecstatic smile, immediately darted around from one place to the other, discovering vital tasks to perform. Emitting a barrage of German like the exhaust from an overheated engine, he explained how to lock and unlock the windows, how to slide the bolt on the door, how to adjust the thermostat.

He was preparing to move on to yet another demonstration when Penny heard her own strangled cry: "*Halten! Bitte!*"

The sharp note in her voice must have frightened him. With jerking nods of his head, he backed out of the room and closed the door.

Penny, biting her lip, stared after him, then sank down on the marvelous mattress.

And promptly forced herself to jump up again.

Stowing her clothes away, she told herself she couldn't go on being so edgy. It was unfair to everyone, particularly herself. She couldn't sour her life, couldn't go on thinking day and night of a man who was obviously busy leading his own life. Pierce hadn't bothered to come down to say good-bye to her. All morning she'd kept hoping, looking over her shoulder right up to the last minute, when the limo arrived to whisk her to the airport.

All right, you fell in love and he didn't love back—an ancient story, she told herself stonily. But you're still you, you're still Penny Marsh. You existed before you knew there was a Pierce Reynolds—you laughed, you sang, you cared about the world. Are you going to throw all that away, turn yourself into a crotchety mess or a blank-eyed zombie? You have a job to do—so get going!

Moving swiftly, she changed her camel blazer to a lightweight blue pullover. Spring was rampant this afternoon in Vienna. She brightened her lipstick only a little. If she got to see Professor Muller, she felt she should look conservative. Then once again she checked through Pierce's instructions, her eyes caught and held by the sight of his dark, bold, modern hand.

Pierce. . . . She would have to train herself not to call him that. Calling him Mr. Reynolds in her thoughts might erect the needed psychological wall between them.

Yes, here it was, Muller's telephone number. Since he lived in the center of Vienna, in what they called the Inner Ring, he might be at home now, at the luncheon hour. She reached for the ornate white and gold telephone.

There was a brief struggle with an operator who knew about as much English as Penny knew German, but eventually the woman seemed to comprehend, there was a buzzing in Penny's ear, and a quiet voice said, "This is Wilhelm Muller. Who is calling, please?"

It was startling, coming so instantly in contact with the man who all along had been just a name. In fact, because of her intense involvement with Pierce, she had given Muller very little thought. She realized now that she had no idea of how she was going to approach him.

"Mr. Muller," she heard her breathy voice, "I'm Penny—Penelope Marsh. I just arrived in Vienna—I'm an American. I . . . I play the violin."

There was a small silence. Then the cultured voice said, "Yes, Fräulein Marsh?"

"I'd . . . I'd like to see you, Mr. Muller. I mean, when it's convenient for you."

"May I ask, why?"

Penny hesitated. If he hung up now, she might never get another chance to talk to him! "It's . . . it's about your violin, Professor. I understand you own a Giuseppe Guarneri."

"Yes . . . yes, that is correct."

"I thought perhaps you'd let me *see* it, Professor! I mean, I've seen only *one* in my whole life, and the one I saw wasn't even playable, wasn't in good shape. I thought perhaps you would permit me to come over and . . . and *look!*"

"I see. You say you are a music student? Who is your teacher? You are perhaps at Juilliard? Curtis?"

"No. I mean . . . I'm not a student. I just . . . play . . . I learned from my father." She held her breath. "My father was David Ernst Marsh."

"David Ernst Marsh. . . . Oh, yes, yes, I remember. . . . But this was many years ago . . . in Philadelphia, I think? *Ja,* I think that was where I heard him once—the Academy?"

"Yes, Philadelphia! That's my home!"

A sigh rustled in Penny's ear. "Well, I wish I could assist you, Fräulein Marsh, but at this moment it is not possible, I am very involved—"

"Oh, *please,* Professor Muller, please just let me see the instrument! I just want to *look* at it! It wouldn't take long!"

"Well, now . . . maybe I telephone you back. Is that suitable, Fräulein? What is your hotel?"

Penny told him. *"Ach, ja,"* he said, "across from you is the Stadtpark—you must go to look at Johann Strauss—he is there with his fiddle— he plays on in the sun and in the snow!"

"Oh, yes—yes, I'll do that! And thank you for being so nice!"

"I will call you between seven and eight, if that is permissible."

Penny said it was indeed permissible, then she

hung up the phone and jumped up excitedly, the small triumph giving her a much needed spurt of pleasure. She remembered her father had once said a person needed work as much as food. It was true. Work was a life saver. When your inner life seemed bare as a desert, work could make a little part of you come alive. . . .

If she could get the violin for Pierce, he'd remember her every time he looked at it. It would be the one thing she could do for him.

But, of course, he wouldn't be keeping it, she reminded herself. Eventually he'd sell it at a much higher price than the professor would get, since the price of fine old violins never stopped going up.

The professor had such a nice voice. It didn't seem to match up with a man who was involved with a flashy model half his age. Still, passion had a way of transforming everyone, and not always for the good.

Penny grabbed up her purse and hurried out of the room. She hadn't eaten breakfast in Paris. She'd been too afraid of missing Pierce and, after he had failed to show, too depressed. Now she was starving, and Vienna was traditionally the ideal place to be when you were in that condition.

The hotel dining room was immense, with a blue and gold ceiling, heavy blue velvet draperies, Gobelin tapestries, a string quartet playing the inevitable Strauss waltz and crowds of people eating immense amounts of food. Every plate that held a fruit or a pastry also held a mound of Vienna's favorite confection— whipped cream.

From a huge menu Penny ordered the only two items she recognized: *palatschinken*—very thin pancakes rolled around ground nuts and apricot jam—and coffee. The coffee wore a high clerical collar—whipped cream, of course, but much sweeter and lighter than any she had ever tasted.

After lunch she strolled past awesome, rather heavy buildings, into the Stadtpark. Under a bower of soft green, spring's unfolding, a marble Johann Strauss serenely played his violin while knots of tourists aimed their cameras at him.

Penny remembered the stories she had read about the unhappy personal lives of musicians. But the same was true of poets and actresses, she realized, and scientists and statesmen, probably every kind of human being.

Lots of people moving around the world lugging broken hearts with them. But somehow they went on living and doing things, sometimes magnificent things.

If only she could keep that in mind! That there were things to live for beside love, small joys that had nothing to do with passion, things like hanging flower baskets, and puddles with rainbows of oil in them, and valentines, and lying in a swing looking up into a tree, and letters from friends—

Couldn't she still enjoy just living, if she

schooled herself to it? Perhaps, eventually, she would even forget Pierce for small patches of time.

Just the thought immediately met with a screaming denial from her heart. Pierce would always be her secret darling, as much a part of her as her name.

If she could just keep the pain at a low level by being busy, busy filling up all the hours.

Determinedly she squared her shoulders and walked on, determinedly she read the historic legends on the metal shields of the buildings she was passing, and fixedly she stared at all the statues.

And tried to pretend she wasn't silently crying.

For two days she sat in her hotel room, leaving only for meals, waiting for Professor Muller to find time to see her. On the second night he finally telephoned. Right after that call, Pierce phoned from Paris.

"I'm seeing the professor tomorrow!" she told him.

He was exuberant that she was getting an audience so quickly. "Now, remember, I've given you a big leeway on price. Sound him out and, then, if you think it's necessary, go the limit. And listen—when you play that violin for him, make it something sentimental and German. How about the *Liebestod*? That always thrills me."

The rest of the conversation had followed

those impersonal lines, and Penny had gone out of her way to keep it like that. At one point, Pierce had said, "What's the matter? You're not sick again, are you? You sound so . . . so lifeless . . . not at all like yourself."

Penny felt a sudden moisture swelling behind her eyelids. Was it possible he had already forgotten that last encounter, that terrible evening when he had called her a tease and she had lashed back as cruelly? Yes, obviously he had completely forgotten. It just wasn't important enough for him to remember.

She struggled to make her voice airy. "It's all the whipped cream they're feeding me here—it has a deadening effect. It's making me fat and satisfied."

"*That* I find impossible to imagine," came the quick, glib answer, dressed up to look like a compliment.

Her audience with Professor Muller turned out to be far less intimidating than she had expected. In fact, Penny found herself thoroughly smitten with the man. He was a neatly shaped gray-haired gentleman with a worn face and lovely sad eyes. Sitting in his high-ceilinged, slate-floored apartment, Penny told him how much she appreciated the chance to see the Guarneri. Gently he had questioned her about her background. If she wasn't a professional violinist, why did she care so much about seeing the instrument?

"Not being a professional doesn't keep me

from loving the violin," she had answered, flushing under the man's keen scrutiny.

In fact, the man's face was so very honest and open that she began to feel immensely guilty about representing herself merely as a violin lover. Suddenly she realized she couldn't skirt the issue, not with this gentle, courtly man.

"The truth is, I'm hoping to *buy* a violin," she admitted. "That's why I want to see yours. Perhaps it will be the instrument I'm looking for—and perhaps I'll be very fortunate and you'll be willing to part with it."

At the outset the professor hadn't been too encouraging. He pointed out that the violin was a family treasure. But then, frowning, he had added, "However, frankly, Fräulein . . . I am in great need of extra money at this moment."

Penny had felt a surge of triumph, thinking of how pleased Pierce would be if she actually brought off the deal.

And she'd felt even more excited a few minutes later when the professor opened the black and silver violin case and sat down to listen to her play the exquisite instrument. Penny knew she was playing well because she was playing with Pierce in mind. The mellow, centuries-old voice of the violin was crying out all she felt for him.

"You have given me a delightful experience, Fräulein," the professor had said, as he stored the violin in its case. "So . . . you wish to buy a fine violin for yourself?"

Penny opened her mouth, but the words "for yourself" snagged her. She hated the thought of lying to this gentle man.

She was spared the necessity for suddenly the door flung open and a girl rushed in, a striking girl with a mane of ebony hair and delicate features knotted in terrible anxiety. "Oh, Willi!" the girl cried, and then let out an urgent rush of German that could only be conveying some disastrous news.

Hurriedly, then, the professor had excused himself, telling Penny he would be in touch with her. And although she felt disappointed at not having sealed a bargain, she had also experienced a sharp sense of relief because she hadn't had to lie to Muller. And it definitely *would* be a lie, telling him she was buying the violin for herself. His girl friend had burst in just in time.

That gorgeous girl—what had Pierce said? "The kind of beauty who wants expensive things and plenty of them. . . ." Funny, the professor hadn't seemed like the kind of man who would turn foolish over a girl young enough to be his daughter.

As she crossed the street and was heading back to the hotel, Penny glimpsed the professor and his gorgeous "Liebes" emerging from the apartment house and climbing into an unusual yellow sports car, the most dashing car Penny had ever seen. One of the "expensive things" the professor was providing his young love?

Love, love, what fools it makes of all of us,

Penny had thought, as the Maserati shot past, bearing the sad-eyed Muller and his ebony-haired inamorata.

After which Penny had gone back to her lonely room to wait. And wait . . . and nap . . . and read . . . and try very hard not to think of anything at all. Particularly anything that could be happening in the faraway City of Light.

Chapter Ten

She waited tensely, but no call came from Professor Muller. After three days she telephoned Pierce Reynolds in Paris, her voice crisp. "I don't know quite what to do now—I don't want him to think I'm a nuisance, but he *did* indicate he was interested, and he *did* say he'd call me back. What do you suggest? Shall I phone him again?"

"Wait till tonight. But be sure to call after the dinner hour, never call a man before his evening meal."

"Yes, Mr. Reynolds." Unconsciously she used the formality she had been deliberately employing in her thoughts—when she remembered.

"What's the 'mister' all about?"

"Well, you know what they say," her laugh was forced, "out of sight, out of mind."

"They also say distance lends enchantment."

"They say all kinds of silly things, don't they?" She made another laugh that caught in her throat.

"You don't sound like yourself. What's going

on? Are you all right?" For some reason his voice had abruptly sharpened.

"Me? I'm having a ball! Good-bye, talk to you later!" Before he could work in another word, she hung up. Then she stood at her window, looking out at the storm that was still bowing the trees. She was remembering, too vividly, the way Pierce's arms had felt the last night she had seen him, the clash and turmoil of her heart. Tears rose in her eyes, and she blinked furiously. This was the second day of steady rain, and being cooped up had left her restless and jittery.

At lunchtime the rain was still falling. On her way to the dining room, Penny had to pass the noisy Danube Café. It was the only informal spot in the hotel, and was much favored by the younger set. It had red-and-white-checked table-cloths, heraldic emblems and a small orchestra that sailed from Cole Porter to thumping polkas with noisy insouciance. Seeing the young people laughing and dancing didn't improve Penny's morale. Sitting down in the big, dark, formal dining room, she only picked at her food. The room seemed made for lonely people like her, people with nothing to do but study a German phrasebook.

Which was precisely what she did for the rest of the afternoon, as the rain pursued *its* dreary routine. The streets were awash, cars sending up heartless sprays, pedestrians indignantly ducking and dodging.

But at last the sullen day was waning and it was time to put in the call to Wilhelm Muller.

She was sure the light, feminine voice that answered belonged to Muller's ebony-haired glamour girl. "Wait, please," the girl said, and then called: "Willi! Fräulein Marsh on the wire!"

The professor sounded strained. "Ach, Fräulein—I am sorry to be so long in calling—a very big personal problem—you will forgive?"

"Of course. I'm sorry you've had trouble."

"*Ja*, trouble. I would like to see you again, Fräulein. Elsa says she will drive to your hotel and bring you here if you are willing? It is so wet, miserable, so you will join us in some *Kirschwasser*—cherry brandy—yes?"

"Wonderful!"

As she plucked up her raincoat, Penny thought about the exotic Elsa, so willing to drive out in a heavy rainstorm—because selling the Guarneri would mean more money for the professor to lavish on her?

She started out of the room—then impulsively plucked up the telephone and put in a call to Paris.

And stood listening to Pierce's phone ringing and ringing and ringing. How silly of her to think she would find him holed up in a hotel room on a spring night in Paris—with the fascinating Anne Martel in the same city!

Downstairs in the lobby a small crowd of tourists was clustered prayerfully at the revolving doors, waiting for the rain to go away. "Wow! Look at that gorgeous hunk of car—a Maserati!" The voice was obviously American.

157

Following the pointing finger, Penny saw the elegant yellow sports car pulling up, with stunning Elsa at the wheel.

It was almost three hours later when Elsa delivered Penny back to the hotel. The relentless rain was still slanting down, and the night's chill had turned the atmosphere into a ghostly white vapor.

As Penny stepped from the Maserati, Elsa impulsively leaned out the window. "It makes Willi so happy that you are the one to buy his violin! He would not want it to go with someone not so nice!"

"Thank you." Penny tried not to show the misery Elsa's words evoked. As the girl drove off, she lingered on the fog-shrouded pavement for a moment, reviewing the events of the evening.

Pierce had been completely wrong about the relationship between the professor and Elsa. It was Elsa's *mother* the professor loved, a woman he had known twenty-two years ago, a woman he had once hoped to marry. A lover's quarrel had separated them, and Elsa's mother had married another man. She and the professor hadn't met again until Elsa's father's death, but almost immediately their love had flowered anew.

"Now my mother finds she needs a heart operation. It is very serious. Mein Gott." Elsa's voice had quavered. "We are very lucky to have Willi Muller. He will take care of her. You see we are very poor."

158

Elsa had gone on to explain that she was an aspiring actress and that even her clothes belonged to her film studio. The Maserati belonged to her producer. "He says someday I will make much money from films, but now we must depend on Willi. The violin will help with the operation, and after he can take my mother to the coast of Spain so she will become strong again. He is a wonderful man, our Willi."

And now, as Penny peered through the fog and headed for the hotel lobby, she remembered Elsa's words, and wished with all her heart that she had never agreed to try to buy that wonderful man's Guarneri.

Because she was deceiving the professor, misrepresenting herself, and it left her with a slow, creeping shame.

The professor wanted his instrument to be in the hands of someone who loved it. He felt about that violin the way someone else would feel about parting with a beloved pet.

But it would be Pierce who would have the violin. Pierce, who would lock it up in his vault and eventually sell it to anyone willing to pay more than he had invested.

And she, Penny, would be guilty of lying to Willi Muller.

If he ever learned the truth, he would mark her down as a salesperson who had pretended to care about music, a dishonest, scheming salesperson.

She felt her shoulders slumping under the weight of her guilt. Disconsolately she squished into the lobby and trudged to the desk for her room key.

"And just where have *you* been?" The words made her head snap around. "What do you mean, behaving like this? Do you realize that you're lucky to be alive, you little idiot?"

Wordlessly Penny stared up at Pierce, standing behind her in the lobby, his dark eyes filled with an inexplicable fury.

Chapter Eleven

"I don't *understand!* What—what?" Penny heard her own mystified voice echo in the almost empty lobby, heard it bounce back from the brocade-paneled walls, while baroque marble angels serenely eavesdropped.

Looming over her, Pierce grasped her arm, his face dark, the expression shattering. "I might have known something like this was going on! I *heard* he was asking around, wanting to know what hotel you were staying in! But I expected you to have more sense!" His lips twisted. "A one-man girl! One man at a time is more like it!"

"What are you *talking* about?" Her teeth were chattering helplessly. "Please, you're hurting my arm!"

His hand fell away then, but his eyes still held their unfathomable, frightening glisten. "I suspected you were too young and impressionable to be let loose in Europe—I didn't realize you were also idiotic!"

"*Idiotic!*" She felt the anger rise, overwhelming her fear. "What do you mean? What right do you have to talk to me this way?"

"Right? I *employed* you! If something happened to you, if they found you lying out there in the road"—he motioned to the door—"it could easily happen on a night like this, with a man who drives like a crazy dervish! Don't you realize that, you little fool?"

The whole world was befogged, dizzying. "Please," blindly she motioned to the lobby chairs, "please . . . can't we . . . ?"

His face lost a little of its fury. Shaking his head, he stalked ahead of her and she followed, weak-legged, dimly conscious that his trench coat was rain-blackened, as if he'd been standing in the deluge for hours. In a vague, stunned way she found herself thinking perhaps he had picked up a virus, was hallucinating from fever. . . .

Tensely she perched on the edge of a chair. He remained standing, staring down at her, his coat dripping rivulets.

"I thought I warned you about him," he said. "I couldn't believe it when I got here and the bellboy told me!"

"Told you *what*?"

"That you'd gone off in that Maserati! I could have killed Genet with my bare hands! He's already been in two bad smashups—don't you remember my warning you?"

Slowly she began to comprehend. She stared up at him for a long moment. When she spoke, her voice was edged with ice. "I met Eric Genet exactly once—at your party. I haven't seen him since. So will you kindly tell me *who* the idiot is, you or me?"

He blinked confusedly. "But I *saw* you! I've been waiting, running out of this lobby every few minutes, looking for that Maserati! I *saw* him pull off and leave you here!"

"Did you? You mean Eric Genet owns the only yellow Maserati in the world?"

Stiffly she unfolded from the chair. Now her anger was controlled, beating steadily in her like a pulse. "Mr. Reynolds, I've just returned from a long session with Professor Muller. Elsa, a friend of his, drove me back here. You'll be interested to know that Professor Muller is agreeable to your price and to the sale. That's all I have to say to you—on a business level."

"Penny—"

"But on a *personal* level," she strode by him, her eyes frigid, "I want to tell you, I don't like you very much, Mr. Reynolds! I don't like anyone who automatically condemns other people!"

"Wait a minute, Penny—"

She pushed roughly past him, past the smiling marble angels, past the open-mouthed desk clerk. As the elevator doors clanged shut on her, tears were streaming down her cheeks, as relentless and exhausting as the rain that continued to drown Vienna.

There was a golden light somewhere, apricot-golden, and a bird sang sweetly. She must be dreaming, because birds didn't sing when the world was drowned in rain, birds wisely stayed mute, heads tucked in their wings. . . .

She opened her eyes slowly and with a start sat up in bed, the sweet dream fading, promptly being replaced by an unhappy memory. Or was the memory also a dream?

No, it *had* happened, abruptly it unfolded, vivid as a play she had just seen and she could recall every word of the cruel dialogue, everything that had been uttered in that midnight-still lobby. Pierce's words, so lacking in trust.

I can't take any more of this, Penny decided. *Today I'll finish all the arrangements with Muller—and then I'll go home.*

Turning then, she saw her bedside clock and gasped, looked to the windows for confirmation—

Afternoon! She had slept a full twelve hours! And the apricot-gold hadn't been a dream after all. A rich day bloomed outside, warm, dreamy, mellow. She heard a child's laugh, caught the sweet, intense scent she couldn't identify of some unknown Austrian flower.

Unfair that it was so lovely! Unfair that the deer would be lifting their delicate limbs in Lainzer Tiergarten, unfair that the sailing boats would be drifting on the Danube and unfair that some people were able to enjoy the soft country hillsides and gold spires of Vienna, while she was wrapped in her cloak of misery.

Once more she found herself reviewing her association with Pierce, and once more she realized that she had often had a sense of some complicated battle going on inside him. But what could the battle involve? He wasn't the kind of man to stumble around, entertain any uncertainties about life's problems.

Oh, she'd never understand him, never get inside him! There had been moments when she had been sure he wanted her physically. Had he told himself it would be too complicated, getting entangled with a girl who was obviously uniniti-ated in the ways of passion?

Or was he so used to easy conquests that a girl who withheld herself became a problem to him? And a girl who demanded more than physical love a real burden?

The more she pondered it, the more depressed she became.

The answer to depression was action so she dressed quickly, putting on the one summer outfit she'd brought, a softly tailored cornflower blue shantung with a scarf in blue, violet and yellow stripes.

When she telephoned Professor Muller, the housekeeper reported he was at the hospital, visiting Elsa's mother. He had left a message that he would telephone Miss Marsh tomorrow.

Penny bit her lip. How terrible if anything happened to Elsa's mother now, when she and Willi Muller had been reunited at last.

Did the joy of love always have to be tinged with sadness?

Downstairs, on her way to the dining room, she turned her eyes from the painful sight of the marble angels in the lobby and met Pierce's dark gaze. He was standing at the dining room door, as if he were waiting for someone. He wore a white blazer over a silver gray shirt and darker gray slacks. Above the handsome outfit his face looked drawn.

"I won't have any news from Professor Muller until tomorrow," Penny said crisply and circled him, eyes firmly fixed on her usual table.

His hand shot out, clamped her forearm. Immediately she halted, and turned a hard challenging look on him and enjoyed seeing his wince. "You're not starting that again, are you—mauling me?"

He sucked in his breath, but kept his hold on her, although his fingers loosened slightly. "When a man is trying to apologize, he is owed an audience."

"All right, let's say you've apologized! Let's let it go at that! I haven't had anything to eat yet, so if you'll please—"

"Look—I have to talk to you, and I can't in this place." With his free hand he waved at the dining room, crowded now with foragers digging into the enormous luncheon smorgasbord.

"It seems to me you've already spoken as freely as anyone could!"

"Penny—won't you be fair?" His eyes were actually entreating. "Fairer than I was to you?"

What would he say, what was going on in his mind? She ached to know. Perhaps it would help her piece together the puzzle that was Pierce Reynolds. And yet a small, sensible part of her warned she should escape while she could.

The trouble was, as she looked up at him, all the other parts of her won the battle. What *was* it about the combination of this man's features, the look in those dark eyes with their heavy eyelashes, that so enslaved her?

"All right," she breathed wearily, "all right."

He tightened his hold on her arm, led her through the lobby to a taxi, and soon they were trundling past the elegant shops on the *Karntnerstrasse*. And because her heart was caught in a web of confusion, tangling wildly at his nearness, she heard herself talking fast, a rush of words about the violin, how beautifully it had been preserved, and about the professor and Elsa's mother—

He held up his hand. "I can't get involved with that at the moment. Not until I make things right with you."

Make things right! It had such a sound of conciliatory patchwork that she suddenly lost all control. "That's something you could *never* do! Do you think a few words can make up for how you treated me last night?"

"Here we go again, fighting every time we meet." He shook his head. "Penny, can't we get along?"

"No—because I can't understand you!" She stared at him, waiting, hoping for some magic word from him that would clear up everything.

He sighed. "I'm having trouble understanding myself."

There he was, fighting his inexplicable battle again. Was it something about Anne? Shaking her head, Penny looked out the window. The taxi had turned into a cobblestone side street. Now it drew up opposite a little plaza with a trickling fountain and a building that looked like a miniature inn, its door painted a gay pink. The taxi driver muttered something to Pierce. "He says the music school at the end of the street is where Schubert studied," Pierce reported. Taking her arm, he started her toward the pink door.

"Where are we going?" she said suspiciously. "If you just want to talk, what's wrong with the park bench?"

He reached up and pulled a wind-tossed strand of hair away from her face. "It's just a little coffee house, you said you haven't eaten. It's a good place to talk, open and sunny—"

Warily she followed him through the pink door, into a room that was more than open and sunny, it was all shimmer and shine, walls paneled in burnished pine, crystal sconces everywhere and small round white marble ice cream tables facing plush upholstered banquettes. Mozart's Symphony Number 40 in G-Minor floated beguilingly from somewhere, and dappled sunlight danced between the lavish sheer ruffles at the beveled windows.

A waitress in a crisp white apron hurried over. "May I order for you?" Pierce said.

"It doesn't matter." Penny was struggling to hold onto her wariness. If only the table weren't so tiny, bringing his knee quite definitely against hers. If only the sunlight didn't make his face so clear and clean and sharp—

Such an exciting face.

Such a *dear* face.

There was a pain in her throat. Tracing the veined marble of the table, she heard him say *"Einspanner,"* saw the tall glass of coffee with mounded whipped cream and powdered sugar appear promptly at her elbow—

"Penny, I've been thinking all night about what I said to you," he said. "Trying to decide how I can make it up to you. I guess all I can do is start from the beginning. You see, when you phoned me in Paris, you sounded very strange, not at all like yourself. And then right after that I got a report that Eric Genet had been asking everyone where the pretty American bébé"—he grimaced—"had gone. Naturally I thought . . . couldn't help assuming . . . well, after all, he *is* the heartthrob of Paris, Anne's told me about his countless affairs."

"I see." Penny kept her eyes on the veins of marble. "And how *is* Anne?" she said lightly. "I'm not sure she would exactly approve of you at the moment—a man with all your involvements, getting all worked up about one little part-time employee."

His eyelids flickered. "I feel involved with anything that happens to someone who works for me."

She looked up at him steadily. "And this is what you wanted to tell me?"

He shifted uncomfortably; puzzled. "If my apology isn't adequate, perhaps . . ." He reached into his pocket. "I know this can't

169

wipe out my boorishness, but when I saw it this morning," he took the small package from his pocket, and put it alongside her plate, "it seemed perfect for you; please tell me if you like it."

Reluctantly she untied the blue moire ribbon. A present. Didn't he realize a present could never change the hopelessness of everything?

But when the wrapping fell away and she saw the exquisite beaded purse, each bead hand sewn to form a striking border for the unique petit point design, she gasped. It was unlike any evening purse she had ever seen.

"It's from Vienna's petit point studios. Remember, I told you about them? I had to go over there to order the chair coverings for Anne."

"Chair coverings?" Penny's hands fell away from the purse. Yes, she remembered how he had talked about the petit point place . . . *Exquisite work . . . chair coverings and the like . . . when I settle down in a permanent home, I'll order from them. . . .*

"Is *that* why you brought me here?" The bitterness rushed up in her. "To tell me about your *chair coverings?* All the pretty details of your home with Anne?" She tossed the beaded purse across the table at him. "Here, give this to Anne, too! It doesn't mean anything to me. It would just remind me of the most horrible time I've ever had in my life!"

She jumped up, but his hand had darted across the tiny table, ensnared her wrist, locked her in place. "Tell me something—why are we jealous of each other?" His voice was low, intense. "Do you know the answer? You are jealous of Anne, and I—" He broke off. "My God, Penny—don't tell me you could be in love with me?"

"*Oh!*" The word was like pain on her lips. "I suppose you want me to say yes to that so you can pity me! Your ego is mind boggling!" She yanked herself free. Blindly she ran through the maze of tables, down the narrow foyer to the pink door.

She ran across the cobblestone street, her eyes wincing against the sudden glare of the sun. There was a taxi near the corner and she sped after it, gasping *"Halten!"*

Then her heel slipped on the cobblestones, and she fell, her foot wrenching sharply, painfully.

"Ohhh!" Bent over, she clutched her ankle, tried to massage it back to normalcy.

"Penny—wait—let me help you!"

Pierce was slamming out of the coffee house and hurrying up the cobblestones in her direction.

Ignoring the throbbing ankle, Penny struggled to the taxi, flung the door open and rasped out the name of her hotel.

Then, as the cab sped off, she sank back in the seat and stared gloomily out at Vienna, its gay sunlight hazed by her inner sadness. Over and over she heard Pierce's words, pronounced with such concerned shock—the way he would talk to someone he was trying to be kind to, someone he was pitying— *My God, Penny—don't tell me you could be in love with me?*

The doctor sent to Penny's room by the hotel manager was a woman with a cold face and a long stiff neck, like an ostrich, but her fingers were gentle, probing the swollen ankle. "No, no need for an x-ray, but we will strap it up. You will have no trouble walking."

"Thank goodness! I have to take a plane tomorrow, I'm going home."

"*Ja,* we always hurry when we are going home," the doctor said, smiling.

Penny gave a wan smile in return. As the doctor went out, the telephone rang again, as it had been doing intermittently ever since she got back to the hotel. Obviously it was Pierce.

Hands clasped tightly, Penny sat listening until the pealing exhausted itself and died out.

After that she dialed the hotel operator. "Please don't put through any calls tonight. I do not wish to be disturbed. *Gute Nacht.*"

"But Fräulein, Room 1420 is calling you many times!"

"I do not wish to be disturbed. *Gute Nacht.*"

To make doubly certain everyone understood, she took the phone off the hook.

Then, as she waited for Room Service to bring her dinner, she sank back on the bed and listlessly leafed through a tattered, year-old copy of *Vienna Highlights,* the hotel publication she had picked up in the lobby. Flipping the pages, her eye caught the headline: OUR FAMOUS

GUESTS. It was a long interview, and alongside it the picture stared up at her. *Pierce*.

The sight of the familiar, angular face was like an arrow to her heart.

By ten o'clock the next morning her suitcase was packed and she had made the telephone call to Professor Muller. It was one of the most difficult things she had ever done in her life, and for some minutes afterward she couldn't stop her hands from trembling.

But ahead of her was a still harder task; briskly she tackled it and dialed Room 1420.

"That was pretty inconsiderate," Pierce said as soon as he heard her voice. "Running off like that, not answering the door, taking your phone off the hook."

"I had to." Her voice was flat. "And now I have to talk to you. I'd appreciate it if it could be as soon as possible."

"Of course. Say—you're not in any trouble with that ankle, are you?"

"No."

"I tried to help you. You just took off."

"Yes."

"We can't even communicate sight unseen, can we?"

"That won't be a problem much longer."

His laugh was dry. "Why not? Is one of us reforming? All right, let's get off that tack. Have you heard from Muller? How's our sale coming?"

"I'll tell you as soon as I see you."

"Your place or mine?" Without waiting for her answer, he added, "We'll make it yours," and hung up.

Penny's heart shook. She didn't want him in her room, didn't want to meet him in such an enclosed, private place. Suppose he touched her? Threw her on *this* bed, too?

I couldn't handle it, she thought, *this time I couldn't resist.* She shivered. Even the brief imagining was stirring her body; somewhere deep within her there was a terrible thirsting, an almost crippling sense of need and frustration.

It was because of all the dreams—every night, against her will, her dreams put her back on that bed with Pierce, made her relive everything that had happened, feel every embrace all over again.

Just five more minutes and it will all be over, she told herself. It wouldn't take much longer than that to tell Pierce what she had to say, what she had told Professor Muller.

Her face burned all over again, as she remembered the Professor's shocked voice. *Then you are not the actual buyer, Fräulein Marsh? The violin would not be for your use . . . your joy?*

The word joy was what had shamed her so. Awkwardly, painfully, she had stammered that she hadn't meant to trick him, that she really loved the instrument and wished so much that she *could* buy it for herself.

Terrible, having to unveil her shoddiness to a man who had really liked and admired her.

174

Pierce's knock cut off her thoughts. She stared at the door, for a moment wondering if she could handle it, if she could do what she had to do. Then she smoothed her face to present a calm appearance—which she was far from feeling— and limped across the room to the door.

Immediately she noticed something different about Pierce, some unnameable change, something she couldn't put her finger on.

But she should be used to that, being puzzled by Pierce Reynolds, she told herself. Besides, it no longer mattered. The curtain was about to fall, the little play reach its sad denouement.

"I wanted to see you, Pierce, because I have to tell you that I phoned the Professor this morning."

"Well, fine. You said yesterday he's satisfied with our price. No change there, is there?"

"*He* was satisfied," Penny said. "But *I* wasn't."

"What does that mean?"

Penny swallowed the dry lump in her throat. "I had to tell him the truth."

"The truth?"

"I couldn't let him go on thinking I was going to be the owner of the Guarneri. I like him, respect him, too much. I couldn't lie to him, Pierce."

"Lie?" His eyes widened angrily. "Who asked you to *lie*? This is a business arrangement. Once Muller sells, it's no concern of his what happens to the violin."

"Just the same, I couldn't do it. I just felt too . . . too fraudulent." She felt tears waiting, but forced them back. "I'm sorry, it just felt too shoddy."

He flushed. "You weren't offering exactly a shoddy price, you know! Anything but. There was nothing even slightly unfair about that deal."

"I know, it's just my own feeling, I can't help it! But it won't change anything for you, Pierce, he's still willing to sell it to you. I . . . I convinced him to go through with the sale. But I don't want to be part of it. I . . . I just have to bow out. As of now."

He looked steadily down at her. "I don't understand any of this."

She turned away. "It's just better this way."

"Better for whom?"

"For *me*. A person has to take care of herself."

"But who's menacing you?" He made an uncertain laugh. "Kindly straighten me out."

"There's nothing to straighten out. I've decided to go home today, as soon as I can get a reservation."

"But that's crazy! You owe me more of an explanation than that." His eyes moved to her bandaged ankle. "You don't need special medical care?"

"No—no. It has nothing to do with my ankle. It's just . . ."

"Just what, Penny?"

For a moment she almost melted under the unexpected gentleness she heard in his voice.

But most good-byes had a quality of gentleness to them.

She felt the sigh going through her like wind in a leafless tree. "I'm sorry. It's just . . . well, this hasn't worked out right since the beginning."

He was silent for a long moment. Then he said roughly, "It hasn't, has it? Strange, the things we can tell ourselves!" He turned away swiftly, his face stiff and blank, utterly unfathomable.

He went out the door.

And out of her life.

Penny sat in the airport's uncomfortable bucket seat and stared numbly down at Pierce's photo, then once again read the *Vienna Highlights* interview with him. It told her some interesting things about his background, things she hadn't known until yesterday. When she got home, she would clip out the photo and story, keep them forever. . . .

Sighing, she tucked *Vienna Highlights* back into her shoulder bag. Then she walked to the waste bin and dropped in her untouched tuna sandwich. Another hour to go till boarding time and she had eaten nothing. No matter how she tried, she just couldn't seem to swallow.

Disconsolately she stared out at the big silver planes taxiing across the runway in the waning sun.

"I never realized a violin could be dangerous to life and limb."

For a moment she thought it was yet another

177

dream about Pierce—Pierce walking toward her, carrying the familiar black and silver Guarneri case!

But the dream was coming too close, looking too tangible. She could see the very real lines fanning out around Pierce's eyes, the faint moisture on his deeply indented lips.

"Did you know a man carrying a violin into an airport is the most suspected character in the world?" Sinking in the seat beside her, he tapped the violin case. "Could turn out to be a tommy gun in here—I've been getting ashen looks from airport personnel."

She was too exhausted to give more than a flicker of a smile. "You're here to tell me you got the Guarneri. I'm glad."

"Of course I got it. Had to, I was given such ecstatic recommendations by a certain highly respected, much-touted young lady."

She flushed. "Not really *ecstatic*—"

"*Ecstatic*," he insisted. "In fact, your admirer, Professor Muller, has been so swayed by you that he even believes *I'm* pretty spectacular, too. He seems to have been given the impression that I am almost saintly enough to have my bust put up in St. Stephen's. Funny, I never suspected I rated that high with you."

"It was just talk—"

"Apparently you did quite a lot of talking. Didn't you tell him that I donated an instrument to that young Viennese pupil they think might grow into another Strauss? How on earth did you find out about that?"

"It was in *here*." Penny pulled out the copy of the hotel magazine. "This article. I just mentioned all that because I thought it would make Willi . . . Professor Muller . . . realize that you respected music! I thought it might make up for all the trouble I've caused you."

"Who said you caused me any trouble?"

Penny looked away without answering.

"Penny." He reached out and steered her chin in his direction. "Look at me—listen to me. *You were right*. About telling Muller, I mean. I was asking you to do something that wasn't part of your character. It *was* a kind of deception, even though it's the kind of thing that's done in my business every day in the week. I see why it would bother you, you react so deeply and personally to everyone you deal with, and apparently they react that way to you."

"Oh, it doesn't matter, now." She heard her listless voice. "You have the violin, that's what you wanted."

"What I wanted," he said testingly. "I wanted something else, too . . . only I didn't realize it until yesterday when you ran away from me and left me standing in the middle of the street."

"I don't know what you mean."

"I think you do. You can't cross the street on your own without getting into trouble—"

"Thanks!"

"—but generally speaking, you're a fairly intelligent creature."

"Please, I'm not up to any arguments right now."

He shook his head. "What a pair we are!"

"Pair!" The ironic, painful word stirred her to infuriated life. "I'm not aware of being part of any *pair*, certainly not one that has you in it! Besides, aren't you pretty thoroughly paired already, paired *and* chaired?"

"Paired and . . . ?"

She could feel her eyes sparking. "You and your petit point chair coverings! Why aren't you with Anne now, why aren't the two of you sitting on your petit point chairs and cooing sweet nothings to each other? You said you never wanted to lose her. Well, why aren't you with her? Why are you following *me* around?"

"I never want to lose her friendship." He sighed. "I never realized Anne was entertaining more complex ideas. I never guessed until that birthday party—until she went to such extremes to get me back to Paris. I felt shocked . . . and then guilty when I realized what she had in mind. I even tried to convince myself that I ought to be settling down with a capable, interesting woman like that . . . so close to my own age. That's why I stayed behind, thinking I could pound some sense into myself, get to see things Anne's way, face the fact that the years were flying by as she so sweetly and frequently pointed out. And, of course, she was right—*is* right."

"Since she's so right and so capable and interesting and wonderful," Penny rushed, "what's your problem?"

"You wouldn't think there would be one,

would you? Another plus is, the lady never fights with me." His hand went out, once again steering her face toward him, and this time the fingers lingered, traced the outline of her mouth. Under his touch she had to struggle not to cry out. "And I never felt a shred of jealousy if she danced with another man, or rode in somebody's racing car. *Because* I didn't feel any jealousy or suspicion, I figured maybe I *was* in love with her. How could jealousy and suspicion be part of love? It's all craziness."

"Craziness?" Penny stared at him, realizing now what was new about his face. There was resolve written on it and also a strange, flaring excitement.

"Certainly, you should trust the person you love, shouldn't you? The only trouble was, I just couldn't feel with Anne what you told me love had made *you* feel."

"What *I* told you?"

"You remember? You gave quite a dramatic description. You said you went around all the time wanting to tell the man you loved that you loved him. 'It just *clamors* at your lips' was the way you put it."

Penny looked mutely at him.

Now his eyes took on a glittering intensity. "You also said you could tell by a kiss. Well, I've kissed Anne."

It was a knife plunging in her. "Oh, I'm sure you have!"

"Nothing, no magic, not a drop. Then I came to Vienna and saw you again and felt that terrible surge of jealousy when I thought you were with Genet. Which brought me face to face with what I'd been trying to deny—that I felt no passion for Anne. Those chair coverings that bother you so, they were a gift that I hoped would make up for the fact that I wasn't interested in what Anne had to offer, her 'love'— although actually 'affection' would be a better word. I didn't want affection. I wanted what I was sure I could have with you, if you weren't already taken."

Penny stared at him, unable to believe what she was hearing. "What is that, Pierce, *what* could you have with me?"

"The excitement of vivid love. The blazing excitement of it—I know now it can't be duplicated—it's either there or it isn't. And I know you'll always excite me. I could swear to it!" His hands went out, closed on her shoulders. "Haven't you seen how I've had to fight to control myself?"

"The excitement you're talking about a man can feel very easily for anyone, anywhere."

"Do you really think I'm talking about just simple desire? About just your beauty, your outward desirability? Yes, that part of you drives me crazy—and at first I told myself that was all it was, but it's much more than that, much more than your beautiful shimmering hair and your eyes and your body—"

She couldn't look away from him—every inch of her was cold, shivering under a shower of delight.

"What really holds me, keeps you in my mind, is your honesty . . . and your idealism . . . the inner part of you that I've occasionally glimpsed." Pierce's eyes traveled caressingly over her face. "And yet I couldn't come to grips with all the jealousy and suspicion I felt. . . . I still can't. Are they part of love? I honestly don't know. I only know I never felt them in relation to anyone else. You wouldn't happen to have the answer, would you?"

"They're part of love, Pierce—the uncertain part," Penny said softly.

"Uncertain?"

"Oh, Pierce, until you're sure the person you love is yours, you can't believe you'll ever have the good fortune to be loved in return! You just . . . you just go around doubting it could ever happen. How could this miraculous person actually share your feelings? You're jealous because you're so uncertain and so afraid such happiness could never really be yours!"

His eyes held a wonderful new tenderness. "You're such a wise little pixie. I think last night I sensed some of what you're telling me. I was lying awake and you wouldn't go away, you were filling all the corners of my heart and brain, and yet I couldn't bring myself to reach for the phone and *tell* you. I had gotten into the habit of holding back everything I felt for you."

Penny lay her hand gently along his cheek. "Why, Pierce?"

He lowered his heavily lashed eyes. "I was afraid you might laugh."

"Laugh?"

He shrugged. "Something Anne said . . . about how young you looked standing alongside me. Oh, it wasn't put that crudely, but I got the drift, and I couldn't help wondering if *you* saw it that way, too."

"If you'd looked in my eyes, you'd certainly have known better!"

"Then, of course, you had told me about the one man you would love forever and I knew enough about you to know you meant it, you'd never change, never desert him for me."

"Him? Oh, Pierce Reynolds, you . . . you *idiot!*" She was laughing, crying, and she didn't care. She'd never have to hide her feelings from him again. *"You* were the one man—from the first day, the first instant. Didn't you *see* it—didn't you *feel* it?"

"Sometimes. . . . But I told myself I was deluding myself. How could you possibly be interested when you constantly spurned me? I was one big turnoff—and that's a direct quote, remember?"

She lowered her head, feeling an unaccustomed shyness. "It's not easy . . . letting a man see things . . ."

"And then you were so young . . ." He looked away from her.

Penny stared up at him. "Pierce, *I'm* the one who's old, *really!* When I'm not with you I shrivel up, I turn mean and sour. I yell at bellboys and when I look in the mirror I see a long, angry, frustrated face!"

"Then I'm laying down a law. As of this moment I expressly forbid you to be away from me for even half a day." For a moment the familiar arrogance was back. "By the way, your professor was wiser than both of us. When I told him I wanted to give you a very special gift, he wasn't in the least surprised. I gather he got the feeling just from hearing us talk about each other that there was something rather strong passing between us."

Penny's eyes widened as he raised the violin case—and then gently lowered it onto her lap.

"Here, your bridal gift, Mademoiselle. You may hold it for precisely one minute. After that I want my chance to hold the bride."

"Bridal . . . ?" Disbelievingly she looked from the Guarneri to him. "Oh, Pierce, I can't take this!"

"You're honor-bound to take it. Muller made me promise as part of the deal you would play for his wedding. But, of course, I'm hoping ours will precede his."

"I'm dreaming! Oh, Pierce, I *must* be dreaming!"

"I'm prepared to provide a very convincing reality." He set the violin case aside. "Come here, young lady."

Penny struggled to stand, and then whispered hollowly, "I can't."

"Why? Your ankle?"

"No—I'm . . . I'm just afraid."

"Afraid?" His eyes went over her face. "Afraid of my love?"

She rose then, moving slowly, as if under hypnotism, and his hands reached for her, circled her, drew her close, and all at once all her fears lifted. His lips touched her forehead and moved slowly, like flitting butterflies, to her eyelids, and then as they found her lips, the honey of his love poured over her, and she was floating, melding into his body. She was bound helplessly to this man she knew she would always love. She closed her eyes, and it seemed to her that she could hear the yearning *Liebestod,* and more than anything she wanted Pierce to hear it too. . . .

"I'm going to play you a love song," she breathed against his cheek. "A very special love song."

"Oh, no you don't. This is one case where the gentleman is first on the bill." He smiled down at her. "You see, I've got a love song I want to play to you—it's one I'm hoping you'll want to hear over and over again."

His grin was suddenly wicked, and Penny, feeling equally wicked as she rested her head against his chest, whispered, "I think you're going to have quite a receptive audience, Mr. Reynolds."

Silhouette Romance

15-Day Free Trial Offer
6 Silhouette Romances

6 Silhouette Romances, free for 15 days! We'll send you 6 new Silhouette Romances to keep for 15 days, absolutely free! If you decide not to keep them, send them back to us. You pay nothing.

Free Home Delivery. But if you enjoy them as much as we think you will, keep them by paying the invoice enclosed with your free trial shipment. We'll pay all shipping and handling charges. You get the convenience of Home Delivery and we pay the postage and handling charge each month.

Don't miss a copy. The Silhouette Book Club is the way to make sure you'll be able to receive every new romance we publish before they're sold out. There is no minimum number of books to buy and you can cancel at any time.

Silhouette Romance

IT'S YOUR OWN SPECIAL TIME

Contemporary romances for today's women.
Each month, six very special love stories will be yours
from SILHOUETTE. Look for them wherever books are sold
or order now from the coupon below.

$1.50 each

Hampson	☐ 1	☐ 4	☐ 16	☐ 27	Browning	☐ 12	☐ 38	☐ 53	☐ 73
	☐ 28	☐ 40	☐ 52	☐ 64	☐ 94		☐ 93		
Stanford	☐ 6	☐ 25	☐ 35	☐ 46	Michaels	☐ 15	☐ 32	☐ 61	☐ 87
	☐ 58	☐ 88			John	☐ 17	☐ 34	☐ 57	☐ 85
Hastings	☐ 13	☐ 26	☐ 44	☐ 67	Beckman	☐ 8	☐ 37	☐ 54	☐ 72
Vitek	☐ 33	☐ 47	☐ 66	☐ 84		☐ 96			

$1.50 each

☐ 5 Goforth	☐ 29 Wildman	☐ 56 Trent	☐ 79 Halldorson
☐ 7 Lewis	☐ 30 Dixon	☐ 59 Vernon	☐ 80 Stephens
☐ 9 Wilson	☐ 31 Halldorson	☐ 60 Hill	☐ 81 Roberts
☐ 10 Caine	☐ 36 McKay	☐ 62 Hallston	☐ 82 Dailey
☐ 11 Vernon	☐ 39 Sinclair	☐ 63 Brent	☐ 83 Halston
☐ 14 Oliver	☐ 41 Owen	☐ 69 St. George	☐ 86 Adams
☐ 19 Thornton	☐ 42 Powers	☐ 70 Afton Bonds	☐ 89 James
☐ 20 Fulford	☐ 43 Robb	☐ 71 Ripy	☐ 90 Major
☐ 21 Richards	☐ 45 Carroll	☐ 74 Trent	☐ 92 McKay
☐ 22 Stephens	☐ 48 Wildman	☐ 75 Carroll	☐ 95 Wisdom
☐ 23 Edwards	☐ 49 Wisdom	☐ 76 Hardy	☐ 97 Clay
☐ 24 Healy	☐ 50 Scott	☐ 77 Cork	☐ 98 St. George
	☐ 55 Ladame	☐ 78 Oliver	☐ 99 Camp

$1.75 each

☐ 100 Stanford	☐ 105 Eden	☐ 110 Trent	☐ 115 John
☐ 101 Hardy	☐ 106 Dailey	☐ 111 South	☐ 116 Lindley
☐ 102 Hastings	☐ 107 Bright	☐ 112 Stanford	☐ 117 Scott
☐ 103 Cork	☐ 108 Hampson	☐ 113 Browning	☐ 118 Dailey
☐ 104 Vitek	☐ 109 Vernon	☐ 114 Michaels	☐ 119 Hampson

$1.75 each

Silhouette Romance

Coming next month from
Silhouette Romances

Dreams From The Past by Linda Wisdom
Kelly went to Australia to fulfill a promise to her father, to see the woman he had first loved, Maureen Cassidy. How could she have known that in Maureen's son Jake she would find a love to last forever?

A Silver Nutmeg by Elizabeth Hunter
Judi Duggan had gone to Spain to design and stitch the trappings for the Arnalte family chapel. She didn't plan to meet the handsome Don—and she certainly didn't plan to fall in love!

Moonlight And Memories by Eleni Carr
Helen had dreamed of a chance to spend the summer in Greece. But the presence of deep, mysterious Demetrios Criades unsettled her. Could she unlock the passions hidden in the chambers of his heart?

Lover Come Back by Joanna Scott
One night of love made her his forever, bound by memory—and a child. Linda tried to escape, but how could she resist this master of the dangerous game of hearts?

A Treasure Of Love by Margaret Ripy
From the moment she met him, Marnie Stevens regretted signing on as Damon Wilson's underwater photographer. But with a will as steely as his penetrating gray eyes, he demanded fulfillment of the contract—in every way!

Lady Moon by Heather Hill
Maggie Jordan had come to the English countryside to restore Deane Park—a vast, Georgian estate. But after meeting its aristocratic owner, she realized the real challenge would be the man, not the job!

READERS' COMMENTS ON
SILHOUETTE ROMANCES:

"I would like to congratulate you on the most wonderful books I've had the pleasure of reading. They are a tremendous joy to those of us who have yet to meet the man of our dreams. From reading your books I quite truly believe that he will some-day appear before me likc a prince!"

—L.L.*, Hollandale, MS

"Your books are great, wholesome fiction, always with an upbeat, happy ending. Thank you."

—M.D., Massena, NY

"My boyfriend always teases me about Silhouette Books. He asks me, how's my love life and natu-rally I say terrific, but I tell him that there is always room for a little more romance from Sil-houette."

—F.N., Ontario, Canada

"I would like to sincerely express my gratitude to you and your staff for bringing the pleasure of your publications to my attention. Your books are well written, mature and very contemporary."

—D.D., Staten Island, NY